Praise for *SaltWater*

'I really loved "Dancing on Canvey". A gem of a tale.'
– Bernard Cornwell, novelist

'The sea shimmers through *SaltWater*, as threatening and beautiful as many of the characters who walk the pages. A gorgeous collection by a bright talent.'
– Nuala Ní Chonchúir, author of *Mother America*

'Lane Ashfeldt is an author of remarkable power.'
– *Sunday Tribune*

'Ashfeldt's stories are love stories to disparate coastal landscapes; the language she uses to describe them is the language of love, the grá she has for the sea. However, she also has an intrinsic feeling for the rhythm and tension and pacing that makes a good story. It is the steady shiver of dread which permeates *SaltWater*, ensuring that we can never be quite at ease, can never sit back and enjoy the scenery, which gives the collection its edge.'
– *Necessary Fiction*

'At the heart of a good collection is damn fine storytelling, something Lane Ashfeldt excels at.'
– *Writing.ie*

'*SaltWater* serves notice of a fresh and original talent. One that we will surely be seeing more of in the years to come.'
– *Wales Arts Review*

Published in 2014 by
Liberties Press
140 Terenure Road North | Terenure | Dublin 6W
Tel: +353 (1) 405 5701
www.libertiespress.com | info@libertiespress.com

Trade enquiries to Gill & Macmillan Distribution
Hume Avenue | Park West | Dublin 12
T: +353 (1) 500 9534 | F: +353 (1) 500 9595 | E: sales@gillmacmillan.ie

Distributed in the UK by
Turnaround Publisher Services
Unit 3 | Olympia Trading Estate | Coburg Road | London N22 6TZ
T: +44 (0) 20 8829 3000 | E: orders@turnaround-uk.com

Distributed in the United States by
IPM | 22841 Quicksilver Dr | Dulles, VA 20166
T: +1 (703) 661-1586 | F: +1 (703) 661-1547 | E: ipmmail@presswarehouse.com

ISBN: 978-1-909718-34-0
2 4 6 8 10 9 7 5 3 1

A CIP record for this title is available from the British Library.

Cover design by Liberties Press
Internal design by Liberties Press

SaltWater

Lane Ashfeldt

Contents

'Dancing on Canvey'
winner of the Fish Short Histories Prize
first published by Fish Publishing

'Catching the Tap-Tap to Cayes de Jacmel'
winner of the Global Short Story Prize,
first published in 'A Lime Jewel'

The Boat Trip

'So, have you made your mind up yet?'

'About what?'

'About the boat trip on Sunday, what else?'

Elizabeth sets her embroidery hoop on the window ledge and winces at the dark thumbprint on the white flowers. 'I didn't even ask my mam. Did you?'

'I did.'

'And will she let you go?'

'She will of course. Sure John Daly's the best skipper on Cléire.' Róisín laughs. 'I know he's my uncle but it's the honest-to-god truth.'

Out over Roaring Water Bay, wind-stretched clouds sail high above Sherkin and Cape Clear Island. At this hour the water in the bay is not roaring at all, but is calm as glass, and fishing skiffs dart across it to set their nets. Elizabeth becomes aware of Róisín standing next to her.

'Isn't it gorgeous?'

'It is. But not so lovely I'd marry a fisherman to keep sight of it. I'd rather a view of the shops in Cork city.'

Elizabeth has her sights set on marrying well and living in a townhouse so grand it takes a dozen maids to clean it. Róisín swore once to do the same; the two of them would be neighbours and would take high tea together while their husbands were out. But since one of the Cotters started courting Róisín, she's changed her tune.

'No one said a word about marrying a fisherman, Elizabeth,' Róisín is saying now. 'It's just a day out, that's all. A bit of fun. You must be mad if you won't come.'

The bedroom door bursts open and Nola hurtles in. 'Won't come where?'

The older girls exchange glances.

'Nola! What did I tell yourself and Maura?'

'To knock and wait. But I've no time, Mam sent me on an errand to say your friend should be getting home.'

'You cheeky little—'

'She's right,' Róisín says. 'Ma'll be praying for me if I'm not back. Best not risk her wrath, not till after Sunday.'

It is Thursday before Elizabeth mentions the boat trip. She is off to the shop to get a few messages, and Mam has come with her to settle the account. As they pass Salters, a low whistle comes from the Fisheries School, the tall stone house by the harbour where children learn how to fish and mend nets. Elizabeth's trips to the shop often arouse the interest of the boys from the school, and she's in the habit of walking by without so much as turning her head. Mam, however, is incensed.

'Ill-bred rapscallions! Treating you like a common hussy. I've a good mind to give out to their teachers.'

Elizabeth's cheeks go pink. The young men busy themselves with their painting, but Mam is not done.

'Blessed school! It's a mystery to me why they keep sending

droves of ragamuffins from all over Munster to fish the Baltimore seas dry.'

'It isn't the lads' fault. They only come because they're sent to learn a trade.'

Mam pauses with one hand on the shop door. It's an equal mystery to her why one of her daughters is thought prettier than the rest. But this one was always a careful dresser. As a child she'd beg for a lace collar or a ribbon. Now she's sixteen and ripe for marrying, Elizabeth's talk is not of ribbons but of moving to the city, and Mam is less keen on giving in to her whims.

'You're awfully well informed about the Fisheries School, of a sudden.'

'Róisín tells me about it. Her uncle is a skipper from Cape Clear, and he teaches the boys.'

'Mark my words, girl, it's one thing to know a skipper. Quite another to be associated with a common seaman.'

'I've no interest in any sailor, Mam. Why, Róisín asked me out on a fishing boat with her uncle and his pals next Sunday — did I even ask if I might go? I did not. I knew you'd get hold of the wrong end of the stick.'

Mam says nothing. She is picturing the delighted face on Róisín's mother the other day when she let it out that her daughter is being courted by a fellow in the fishing industry. 'A local man, thanks be to God.' If only Elizabeth too would land herself a Baltimore man with a good living, perhaps she'd forget this codology she's got into her head about leaving for Cork city.

Later, Mam asks who is to skipper this boat, and who else is going? Finally, once she's sure there's no harm in it, she says, 'Why did you not come to me sooner?'

By suppertime it is all settled. Elizabeth is surprised by Mam's approval of the boat trip. Confused, even. Has someone told her one of the men is a catch, is that it? But if that were it she would say. Besides, if Róisín is right the only eligible young man aboard will be her Mr Cotter.

Elizabeth draws the curtains. She pauses a second and notes how swiftly the October night has closed in. Just a hint of sunset left, a swirl of navy and tangerine sky.

After hearing so much about him, Elizabeth finally meets Dónal Cotter for the first time as they go aboard the fishing boat. The fellow is so huge, he eclipses the tiny Róisín. After a few minutes of awkward three-way chit-chat as the boat pulls out of the harbour, the couple excuse themselves and stand near the bow, eyes shielded against the brightness, while he points out to her the island where his parents live.

Elizabeth keeps an eye on them from where she's sitting, but catches only a little of what they're saying. She notes how happy Róisín looks. She is beautiful. And for the first time she entertains the possibility that perhaps Róisín may not be moving to Cork city with her, after all.

The wind carries back a hint of familiar perfume. Nola, sitting nearby, also picks up on the lavender scent.

'I'd say Róisín has borrowed your perfume,' she says.

'She has not.'

'How can you be so sure?'

'I just am.'

The two friends each bought a bottle of the same scent the day they were at the church bazaar together, but the older girl is in no mood to explain. Her sister's presence enrages Elizabeth. It was Mam who let Nola come on the boat trip, as a birthday treat.

Elizabeth feels spied upon with Nola tagging along.

'She might have borrowed it without asking,' Nola insists.

'Róisín is my best friend. She wouldn't borrow one iota from me without asking. In fact, the one person I know who might do that is: well, guess who?'

'Who?'

'Why, you, of course.'

'A nice thing to say. On my birthday, too.'

Nola turns her face to the islands like Róisín and her young man, so her sister will not see the fat tears in her eyes. She forces herself to think of something else: to just watch the islands swim by. Some are so small they are just rounded humps of rock with green seaweedy backs, looking for all the world like undersea creatures that have popped up to the surface to catch a breath of air, and will soon be swimming beneath the waves once more.

When they reach Schull, Elizabeth holds back from entering the public bar with the rest. Telling Róisín and Nola that she'll be along shortly, she goes to the powder room, checks her hair, then scours the hotel foyer and tea room for a sign of a bachelor in a well-cut suit. But the only people under the age of sixty are a man and wife. Although not touching, their two bodies seem connected. Something about them reminds her of the way Dónal Cotter's bulky frame sheltered Róisín earlier.

Elizabeth takes a seat across from the couple, half wishing she'd never come on this trip. She closes her eyes and for a moment it's quiet. Then a voice asks,

'Elizabeth? Elizabeth are you all right?'

'Don't fuss, Nola.'

'I'm only doing as Mam said. You're minding me, remember? I'm to stay with you and do as you say.'

'You're thirteen years old now, Nola. Old enough to mind yourself. Would you ever go on back to the others and leave me be? I've a fierce headache.'

Blinking hard, Nola stumbles back to the bar where the men from the boat are smoking and drinking porter. This is the worst birthday ever: not even a cake.

When Elizabeth opens her eyes again the woman across from her is gone, but the man is still there. He is about the age of Róisín's youngest uncle, in his twenties or thirties, but a city man — you can tell from his suit and his wire-framed reading glasses. He gives a friendly smile.

'You must be a local?'

'Just visiting.' Elizabeth doesn't like to be thought of as a small-town girl. 'I'm moving to Cork city soon.'

'A grand city. You'll love it there.'

'Is that where you're from yourself?'

'It is.' He smiles. 'And what will you do in Cork city?'

She hasn't a clue yet. But it doesn't matter as long as she makes her escape from Baltimore. Baltimore, where everyone in town knows all about you before you even know it yourself.

'I'm not sure. Work in a library, perhaps.'

'As it happens we're looking for presentable young ladies as secretaries at the bank I manage.' He hands her a card. 'Why don't you drop me a line?'

'Thank you, I will.'

Suddenly Elizabeth's world is a brighter place. This last year or so watching girls her own age get engaged, she has seen that she has only one chance at life. If she wants something she must go out there and take it.

The man seems to be waiting for her to leave, so she stands and tucks his card in her purse.

After supper Mam goes up to Elizabeth's room to watch the boat come in. It's a small room but it has a fine view, although it's one she rarely sees, for her eldest daughter finds excuses to keep her out. She fights off the urge to examine Elizabeth's things. Instead she gazes at the rugged coastline, then lies on the bed and closes her eyes. When she wakes the twilight is long gone and her daughter is moving softly about the room.

'There you are. Did you enjoy the boat trip?'

'Mam, it's me, Maura. I came to watch with you, but you were sleeping. There's been no sign of them yet.'

Mam presses her face to the window, dizzy from getting up too fast. Not a star in the sky.

'They swore blind they'd be home before dark.'

'Time must have got away with them,' Maura says calmly. 'I'm sure they'll be back any minute.'

Carbery's Isles are a danger to those who don't know them, but though he is not yet thirty John Daly has trawled these seas half his life and is unafraid, even on a night as dark as this. Last year when a warship blew onto the rocks off Cape Clear, he and two men went out in the storm and pulled forty-five men off that boat alive. The night the Nestorian was wrecked, the weather was magnitudes worse than this: all they're up against tonight is no moon and an ebbing tide. John Daly shakes his head, tries again to find his stars. He doesn't know he is sailing into a mist, a mist so thick the Baltimore fishermen have not gone out.

A few feet away in a world of their own, Róisín and her young man are enjoying the novelty of each other's company. He drapes his jacket around her shoulders; the summer dress picked for this morning's fine weather is little use against the chill evening air. Róisín's eyes glitter and her laughter rings out across the water at some joke only the two of them can share.

Elizabeth, also in a light dress, is feeling the absence of either a waterproof jacket or a broad-shouldered man next to her to ward off the wind. Nola takes a seat beside her. 'I'm freezing,' she says. This time her big sister makes no move to chase her away.

'Please God we're nearly there. I'd say that's Sherkin.'

The shape ahead of them is unclear. A patch of fog blurs things and the dampness of it makes Nola shiver.

'We'll be in fierce trouble over being so late.'

'Don't you worry Nola, I'll handle Mam.'

Maura shakes her mother. 'Mam, come here. I can hear them!' The older woman stumbles to the window, and together they watch for the lights of a boat coming towards harbour.

'Are you sure?'

'I'd swear it's them.'

A smile, 'Ah yes, that's them all right.'

'I wonder what happened the boat's lights?'

'And tell me in God's name why are they shouting and roaring like that? The young hussies, after they promised to behave like ladies. They'll feel the back of my hand when they get home.'

One minute Nola and Elizabeth are thinking of the nice warm beds waiting for them, and the next — crack — everyone on the boat is shouting in a panic. John Daly is trying to steer for the nearest land. Everything goes dark when the engines fail. Nola hears screams and the splash of someone jumping overboard.

She makes a dash for the railing.

'Elizabeth, I'm going to jump.'

Her sister's voice in the darkness,

'Don't you dream of it, girl.'

As Nola climbs the rail the deck tilts like a swinging-boat at the funfair and she can hear things breaking, people falling and shouting. There's no time. She has to do this. Now. She leans out as far as she can, takes a deep breath and lets go.

A splash, a shock of cold, a numbing blackness. And the quietness of it, like she'll never hear anything again. Then the thumpety-thump of the blood in her veins. Nola's chest tightens. Her mouth opens and air bubbles gallop past her ears and break on the surface. Her face follows and water hisses out of her ears. From above, a barrage of men's shouts cancel each other out.

In the muddle, her sister's voice is sharp and clear:

'Nola! Get back on board this instant, you hear me?'

How? She can't even see the boat. Nola tries to cry for help but only coughs salty water. Elizabeth was right: she should have done as she was told. Someone grabs her roughly and pulls her away. A rock looms from the depths like a totem, and the hand on her shoulder pushes her towards it.

'Elizabeth,' she yells as she grabs the rock, 'I'm safe.'

No answer.

'Elizabeth! Jump in.'

But Nola gets no reply.

They are still clinging to the rocks when an awful silence tells them the boat has gone down. A swell washes over the rock, and it tugs as if to pull her into the deep. Nola holds tight. When the water loosens its grip, she climbs higher. Someone starts the rosary and the rest of them join in. Nola feels colder than she's felt in her life, and tired enough to let go. She tries not to think, to just say the responses in a rhythm with the rest.

Some days later when Nola has left the house just the once to attend the Mass for her sister and those who did not make it home, a man from the local paper knocks on the door. Her mother fetches her from her bedroom. Nola is not keen but Mam insists: 'It will do you good.' She brings a pot of tea into the front room and says, 'I'll leave you to it, so.' Her face attempts a smile but the eyes do not match. They look distant, as if she cannot quite focus on Nola. The door closes behind her and Nola hears her go upstairs again, back to Elizabeth's room.

Nola answers the questions as well as she can. By the time she has told the newspaper man about the islander who woke up thinking he was hearing angels, and who rowed out and fetched them in from the rock, it seems to her as if her birthday was years ago, not days. And she is gripped by a fierce cold, just like when she was clinging to that rock.

'I'm a facts man. No good with superstitions or what ifs.' The newspaper man closes his notebook. 'No one from the engine room of the *Thomas Joseph* can speak to us now, so we'll never know for sure what happened. But the fact is, Nola, you're here. And you're alive.'

She shivers.

He says softly, 'Make the most of it now, won't you?'

SaltWater

Tobacco
The taste of tobacco filled his mouth and made it water. Jim spat, and he felt ready for the sea again. You had to be ready for the sea because, if not, then the sea would be ready for you.

He tucked the tin of tobacco away in his pocket next to a smaller one: snuff. A habit learned long ago. On his first voyage they crossed the Mediterranean, a sea warmer and calmer than any he'd known, then stopped in Istanbul to deliver one cargo and load the next before sailing across the Black Sea to the Sea of Azov. Jim was sixty now and had forgotten who it was had passed him some snuff and shown him how to use it, he just knew that by the time he came home he had his own tin.

Jim's wife, Nola, didn't mind him smoking a pipe, but she disapproved of snuff so he never touched it at home. At sea he took a pinch now and again. One peck and his eyelids would be taped open for hours.

Brown cake
Friday dawned bright and clear. A perfect day for the Silver Strand. And yet when her daughters begged to take the ferry to Sherkin Island, Nola refused. She turned off the wireless and

banged about in the back kitchen washing clothes, while her two youngest splashed each other in the curtains of water that fell from the mangle.

Next, Nola chased the younger ones outside to play and got out her baking bowl.

'Can't I stay, Mam, please?' Rosannah asked.

'I'm busy now, child.'

'But I want to learn how to bake a brown cake.'

'Copy me, so, if you want to learn.'

Nola pulled on her apron. She flung ingredients into her bowl: two cups of brown flour, one of white; knob of butter, spoon of soda, pinch of salt. She made a well in the middle and filled it with buttermilk. A quick stir and the dough was soft and springy as it should be.

But when her daughter tried, flour smoked out of her bowl and frosted the table. Nola took over briefly: a drop more buttermilk, a lick of the wooden spoon, and Rosannah's dough came together. She watched while her daughter kneaded it and set it on the baking tray.

'Don't forget to make a cross.'

'Why do you make a cross on brown cake?'

'You just do.'

'But why?'

'To keep you safe.'

'How can a cross on a loaf of bread keep you safe?'

No answer. Rosannah scored the lines on it all the same, and the two rounds of dough sat side by side on the tray: one smooth, the other lumpy and fragmented. Soon the tray disappeared into the range and the scent of baking bread filled the house.

Four mile offshore

It was hard on Nola him being away so much, and these last years Jim had travelled no further than Wales if he could avoid it, to spare his wife the worry. Even going that far was not without its risks now, thanks to the war.

'You're never sailing for England?' Nola said.

'Only as far as Cornwall to pick up a load of china clay for the Arklow Pottery.'

'Did you not hear they'd bombs right along the south coast of England? I saw it on the Pathé News at the cinema.'

He'd heard alright. Still, you had to put bread on the table somehow. 'Don't worry yourself, girl. Those planes haven't the range to fly out west.' Nola said nothing in reply but made a clatter as she went about cleaning the house. Jim hoped now it was true what he'd told her.

Loading at Par was not too bad once their turn came. They opened the hold, hooked a chute on the derrick, and shovelled the clay into it, the weight of it making the boat settle in the water. Jim left Hegarty and Jerome at work and hurried to the post office. Once he sent his telegram to Nola they could be on their way. He passed up the chance of a berth for the night in the hope they'd get home sooner by making a night crossing.

The land hereabouts had a lovely softness to it in the evening light. It would almost pass for West Cork, but he would be glad now to see the back of Cornwall, all the same. He took care to keep four mile offshore, in international waters, because of the emergency rules.

Towards dawn when the Longships Lighthouse was behind them, he set an easterly course and passed the wheel to Hegarty.

Swans and trains

Rosannah tucked a few stale crusts in her pocket and went out back. At the end of the garden she leaned out over the gate and hurled the crusts in the river for the swans. Back indoors, her big sister Mara scolded her: 'There you are. Get a move on, will ye, or we'll miss the train to Baltimore.'

'But Mam said—'

'She'd a telegram from Daddy, and she changed her mind.'

As she fetched her swimsuit Rosannah wondered, what present would Daddy bring? Last time it was pink sticks of rock, the letters 'A PRESENT FROM SWANSEA' running through the minty stick. They hurried up North Street, turned right at the square. At Bridge Street, Nola glanced behind her to check all her children were there. She'd lost Billy. She spotted him in the square by the Maid of Erin statue, chatting to some pals. 'Mara, will you ever run back there and tell Billy from me if he misses that train he'll be locked out for the day. That'll shift him.'

Mara and the girls took seats together and Nola took a single nearby. Billy went into the next carriage, perhaps to smoke an illicit cigarette. Nola had forgotten her knitting, so she contented herself with gazing out at the Ilen, the same lazy trickle of a river that ran behind their house in North Street.

'Mammy, are we nearly there?' Rosannah asked.

'Not long now.'

'We will go swimming, you and me, won't we?'

'Yes darling,' Nola said, distracted.

Skiffs and planes

On Hegarty's watch a light swell held them back. Jim swore softly as he took the wheel. If they'd made better speed they'd be closer to Wexford than Wales by now. When they hit a light easterly he gave the order to hoist sail. It would help make up for lost time.

The seas were awful quiet these days. It was the small boats Jim missed, the one or two man fishing skiffs going about their business at dawn and dusk, and the sailboats darting out to the nearest rock and back for regattas. But bigger ships, too, were down in numbers.

When Jim first heard the planes he wasn't worried. Yes, there was a war on, but it wasn't their war. You'd only to see the Irish flag on the mast and you knew that. Still, the noise grew louder.

Jerome ran into the wheelhouse. 'Three German fighters.' His voice wobbled. 'Coming right at us. Christ, what'll we do?'

As captain, Jim was meant to have all the answers. He had none. The pilots had to leave them out of this — they just had to. The planes came in low over the Loch Ryan, looking so graceful it was hard to imagine they might be dangerous.

Jim sent up a silent plea-bargain to the pilot. He was near enough to see the flag. No question. The question was, what was he going to do about it?

Hardboiled eggs in silver paper, with sand

The 'Dún an Óir' only carried two dozen passengers and by the time they reached the pier it was full. But the skipper, Mikey Taidghín Ó Drisceoil, found a way to squeeze Nola and her family aboard. It was only a short stretch over to Sherkin, after all. And an easy stretch, too. Due south. Going west was where it got tricky; out towards Schull where the sea was peppered with dozens of small islands and rocks that you'd to keep in mind at high tide when they lurked beneath the surface.

On the middle stretch a younger man took the wheel and the

skipper went around collecting fares. Nola held out the fare like she always did, and like always Mikey Taidghín said, 'You're all right, Nola. Enjoy yourselves now, and next time don't stay away so long.' This gave her a warm feeling: somehow, against the odds, he still held her to be 'a local'. If the day ever came when he let her pay the full fare, she'd know then that she really had stayed away too long.

The boat slowed as they approached the harbour, and bumped gently against the pier wall. Passengers clambered up stone steps softened and rounded by year after year of waves. The children ran on ahead of her, up past the abbey and over the hump of the island. Nola was last to reach Trabawn. She sat down heavily and asked Mara to keep an eye on the little ones while she got her breath back.

Rosannah stamped her foot when her swimsuit was on. 'But you said you'd come in for a swim, Mam, you said.'

'I said no such thing. Now you run along and be a good girl for Mara.'

Mara took her little sister by the hand and they set off for the shore. Their voices drifted back.

'Don't be silly. You know Mammy doesn't swim.'

'Why not?'

'When she was a girl not everyone learnt to swim.'

'Why?'

'Because.' Mara said the word firmly, borrowing some of her mother's finality.

Their voices faded and their swimsuited bodies shrank to small blobs against the glare of the water. Nola laid the beach towels over the refreshments bag for lack of shade; it was a scorcher of a day. The towels mounded over the bag made a tempting pillow. No need to worry about crushing sandwiches, for she'd brought none. If the children were hungry after their swim they'd have a hardboiled egg each. Soon Nola was curled up, half asleep. In the distance the children argued over who had the ball and whose turn it was for the float, and over other issues that to them were the most pressing in the world.

China clay

The planes swooped in so low that they almost tipped the mast. Jim tried to alter course but with a heavy load of china clay in the hold, the schooner handled slow and clumsy. Easy prey. He kept his hand on the wheel until the sound of it came.

Ack-ack-ack! Ack-ack-ack!

All three of them ducked. The wheelhouse window shattered and a hail of glass fell over them. Jim tasted bile in his throat. Meanwhile the boat gently, pointlessly, swung around.

To the men cowering on the wheelhouse floor it seemed an age until they'd a chance to take cover. While the planes were turning to make ready for a fresh attack, the three men made a dash for it and scuttled below deck. Jim was last man in. Ears ringing, he slid down the handrails, his feet touching nothing until they slammed into the boards.

'At least now we've an iron deck and two inches of planking between us and them guns,' he said.

'What do we do now?' Jerome asked.

'Sit tight,' Hegarty said.

Famous last words. Because that's when the bomb blew off the hatches.

It wasn't the first bomb the planes had let fly, but the others had only boomed in the water. This one broke through the deck to land in the hold. The bulkhead rattled, and a fearsome thunder shook the whole craft. Wisps of smoke curled around them.

'Mother of Christ,' Jerome said. 'What'll we do if she breaks up on us?'

Jim bit his lip. A man who had been at sea as long as Hegarty or himself knew better then to say such things aloud. All he said was, 'She's stout built, lad, she'll not break up easy.' But inside he was thinking: this could be the finish of us.

Salt

The children's calls and whoops echoed over the sleeping Nola. She too had once played on this strand as a child. Those long summer days, the smallest thing was enough to colour each moment: who caught the most shrimps, who stood in a cow-pat, who built the biggest sandcastle, who drank the last drop of water — the constant three-legged race of being part of a large family.

Sand worked its way under her nails, sun licked a red patch on her neck, but Nola felt none of it, for in her dream she was once more in Baltimore. Baltimore on a bright autumn day wearing its gladrags, a day that fooled everyone into thinking it was still summer. 1918, the week of her birthday, the day of the boat trip. She'd fought hard for a place on that boat and only thanks to her birthday had she won. All that pleading, and the trip to Schull was over in hours — ending with the ugly crack of hull on rock as the boat hit the Catalogues.

Nola's face twisted in sleep. Darkness, the splash of someone jumping overboard. Her call, *I'm going to jump!* And her sister, *Don't you dream of it.* The tilt of the deck, a deep breath, a jump into the dark. Salt in her throat. A hand on her shoulder, a rock underfoot. Listening, but no Elizabeth. Just that awful silence, and the waves.

Nola woke with 'blessed art thou' on her tongue, a tightness to her face from dried tears or sunburn. The accident still upset her, to this day. She glanced around. It was a while since she'd seen the children. She walked towards the waves, squinting to make out their figures against the brightness of the water.

Splinters

Perhaps the pilots thought the smouldering boat was done for, or perhaps they were low on petrol; in any case the planes left. As the engines faded Jim could hear the timbers groaning.

Hegarty took a look outside, gave a low whistle.

'The state of her.'

Plumes of smoke wafted from the hold.

Jerome was on his feet as soon as Jim gave the nod. He rushed up the ladder and ran aft.

Jim felt short of breath as he surveyed the damage for himself. His gaze darted over a deck littered with splinters: chipped masts, torn sails, a wheelhouse and galley all bent out of shape. Holes like a pox on every inch of timber.

Jerome returned slow and grey-faced. 'The lifeboat,' he said. 'It's shot to ribbons.'

Waves

In the shallows, Nola's two eldest were teaching her youngest to swim. Yvonne was playing beachball with a group of friends and Lilly was with her, thank God. So that was Rosannah waving her shrimp net from the far side of the strand. Nola waved as she had to the others, but still the child agitated her net. Why did she keep on waving like that, what was wrong with the child?

She turned, looked back once more, and understood. Rosannah was on a sandbank, and the tide was coming in behind her. She was scared she wouldn't be able to swim back to shore. Nola's pace quickened as she walked towards her daughter. The sea was loud with the incoming tide as she did the very thing she'd feared since her thirteenth birthday. She entered the water.

Sweet dust

Jim felt in his pocket for the smaller tin, tipped a line on his thumb and sniffed it back. If ever there was a time to be alert it was now. He took a deep breath and spoke slowly and calmly so as not to panic the boy.

'If she does break up, lad, we'll grab some timber and build ourselves a raft.'

They joined Hegarty in checking on the hold. Jim looked in wonder at where the clay had lain scattered in lumpy mounds. Now a white dust as fine as sieved flour was settled on every surface. Hegarty was whited over from head to foot. He threw some dust at them, a manic grin on his face.

'Isn't china clay gorgeous? Don't you just love the stuff?'

'What?'

'You all right there, Hegarty?'

A handful of white dust landed on Jerome's chest. He made a dash below, and next thing the two of them were snow-fighting in the hold. When the boy was as white as Hegarty, the two of them fell down laughing.

'Beautiful,' Jim said. 'This is what saved the *Loch Ryan*. All the force of that bomb went into grinding it down. It's a miracle. Not a sign of a leak on her.'

'She looks in need of fixing to me.'

'She's a bit shook alright, but she'll see us back to land.'

Rock

Water crashed against the rocks, then seethed back again. Rosannah looked shorewards, wishing she'd never come on the sandbank. Where was Mammy?

At last, there she was, her dress hitched up, waves cresting her knees, calling out to her. Rosannah strained to hear, but a wave filled her ears with thunder. She was coughing salt water when the next wave hit, churning and foaming until it stole the sandy ground from under her feet, and with her face underwater she lost track of which way was up. Her toes nudged a rock. She pushed down and launched herself up off it, hard. She burst into the brightness and gulped air.

'Hold on!' her mother called, skirts floating around her like seaweed. 'Hold on.'

Remembering her swimming lessons, Rosannah reached out her arms and pulled the water behind her.

'I am holding on, Mam,' she said. 'I am.'

Roaring Water Bay

Auntie Rose was the vintage of the oldest penny that we found buried in our back garden. Born in 1892. She wore her hair in a white bun. She made bread and scones, she planted hyacinths and forsythia, she scolded and comforted, clucked and sweetened. In her late nineties she went 'home' on a visit. Within weeks she was dead and buried in the cramped family grave, as if the land itself had killed her. Only then did I learn of her lost child, the 'sin' that made her leave, and understand why she used to say, defiant: 'They can scatter my ashes over Roaring Water Bay.'

Dancing on Canvey

Adelsburg

Friday morning I stagger up the steep grassy bank of the sea wall on Smallgains and walk along the top, creek to my left, road to my right. The odd wave sends spray flying up, and the wind curls between my legs, snapping at the skirt of my school gabardine.

Archie and his friend Jim try to follow.

'Get down!' I tell them. 'You're not allowed up here.' Nor am I, of course. Strictly speaking.

'I'll tell Mam on you,' Archie yells, and pokes his tongue out at me before running ahead towards school until he's just a small speck down at ground level.

It's weird if you think about it, this island that's not really an island anymore with its tall grassy banks to hold it in place. Even now with the tide not fully in, if the sea were level both sides of the wall it would lap at Archie's shoulders. Maybe his nose, even. Not that you do stop to think of it normally, it's just this thing we've been doing in art has it all fresh in my head.

Brandenburg

Double art last class. Everyone fidgets while the teacher hands out half-finished scrolls. Since Christmas we've been making a frieze of the island. Yellow Table has painted the Danish and Roman remains; Red has made a grassland dotted with cotton wool sheep and a cut-out shepherd. I'm on Green Table. I've sketched the Dutch Cottage with its thatched roof and octagonal base, like a windmill minus the arms. Today I'll colour it in. When Mr Frome hands out sheets of lined paper and tells us to describe what's happening in our pictures, a girl on Blue Table asks will this come up in our 11+. The answer's no.

'But good handwriting,' he says firmly, 'is a skill that will serve you well whatever your future occupation.'

That's when Johnny Deakin starts.

'Soon as I turn fifteen I'll be a fisherman like my dad,' he says. 'Fishermen don't need to read or write, sir. I'd leave school now if I could.'

'That would be your loss,' Mr Frome says, a tight, hard note to his voice.

'All's I need to know is how to sail a boat, how to swim and how to catch fish. And, sir, school don't teach me none of it.'

In maths he'd get the cane for answering back like this. The class goes still waiting for the teacher's reaction. Outside, the red fin of a ship's funnel slides across the sea wall, forming a brief interruption between grass bank and grey sky. Finally Mr Frome speaks. The hardness in his voice is still there, but all he says is that until he turns fifteen Johnny must go to school, no matter how much he wants to catch fish.

Johnny says nothing.

'Why don't you sit on Green for a change?' Mr Frome sets a chair next to mine and hands him a map of Canvey. 'Here. List all the roads with Dutch names.'

It's my first time being on the same table as Johnny Deakin. He is taller than Mr Frome, and strong, and the faint fur on his upper lip either makes him look stupid or like a grown man, depending on the light. I try not to look at his face.

Mr Frome reads a passage about Canvey by the writer of Robinson Crusoe. I listen while I colour in, to his put-on peasant voice that sounds like a radio actor pretending to be from the country. Johnny Deakin stabs at his desk with a compass, denting the wood.

'How should I know which roads have Dutch names? 'S all double Dutch to me,' he says, and in the margin of his page he starts to draw a Spitfire.

'Look by Sunken Marsh,' another boy tells him. 'Half the streets round there end in -burg. When the Dutch got their land they built houses, a church, and everything.'

That's Simon Fairfax. Simon won't be leaving school at fifteen; he wants to go to the grammar and study law.

'Course,' says Johnny. 'They couldn't build dykes all day long, then sail back to Holland at night, could they?'

Mr Frome glares at us.

I whisper road names and point them out on the map for Johnny to copy down. Spelling and Johnny don't get along. Some of the children in my class say he failed his 11+ at his old primary, that he's twelve years old and ought to be at big school. But there's no real way of knowing if this is true. Sometimes I reckon they just don't like being smaller than him.

'Strasbourg, Korndyk, Hilversum, Laars. And Heeswyk, where I live.'

Bent close to the page, Johnny traces the curves of each letter. Even so, from time to time a letter waltzes out of line. I like the look of his alien Ns and Rs.

'Three minutes,' Mr Frome warns.

Quickly, I make some notes.

Canvey's Dutch past
In early C17, experts from Holland came to drain the land
and build sea walls. The Dutch took as payment one third of
the new land, the Third Acre Lands. But later they sold their
land and moved away, and nobody fixed the sea walls
properly. More floods came in 1791, in 1881, and 1897.

Simon Fairfax is watching a point behind me and above my head. A floorboard creaks — Mr Frome. 'Not bad, Johnny,' he says, surprised. I hold my breath as he examines my page. 'Be more precise, Gwynnie. When was the contract signed?'

'1632?'

'Here's a clue: three hundred and thirty-one years ago.'

In my head I take 331 from the current year, 1953.

'1622, sir.'

'Then write it down,' he says.

When he's gone, Johnny Deakin smiles at me. I look away from his brown eyes, but in a way I'm glad I got something wrong because Johnny's told off every single day. At least today he's not the only one.

Heeswyk
Walking up Smallgains on the way home, Archie and Jim argue over who scored the winning goal in some football match. Bored with their —*did* —*didn't* —*did so* —*did not*, I race uphill to the sea and walk along the top of the sea wall. The wind is fierce, the tide further in, though strands of darkened seaweed at the high water line show it's on the ebb. But I'm not thinking about the sea: it's just there, the way it always is. No, I'm not thinking about the

sea, I'm thinking about Johnny Deakin. Trying to work out what it is about those brown eyes of his that makes me uncomfortable. He's strange. I wouldn't want him for an enemy, but I'm not sure I want him for a friend either. As I'm thinking this, a shadow touches me. I turn and he's standing right next to me, even taller than I thought. Taller than my dad, but skinnier.

'Wild today.'

I keep walking, unsure what to say. Johnny Deakin takes the windy side and keeps pace beside me. I don't know where he lives, but I've never seen him walk home from school this way before. His family's new to the island, that much I know. Last year when they moved out from Bethnal Green someone said his dad was a docker.

'Is your dad really a fisherman?' I ask.

'Weekends he is. Mostly we fish off the sea wall over by the Lobster Smack. But his best mate has a boat and sometimes we go out with him.'

On the pavement below, Archie and Jim join hands and mince along together, then turn about-face, pointing and laughing at us. Johnny hasn't seen. He's facing seawards, eyes narrowed against the horizon.

'Another high tide tonight,' he says.

'How d'you know?'

'Moon's just off full. They'll be gawping at it on their way to the dance tomorrow.' He laughs, then looks me in the eye. 'You going? Nah, you're too young, int you?'

He hurls a stone in the water.

'It's not that. I might, I just . . . don't know yet.'

He starts down the slope. Veering towards his own house, I suppose. When he's most of the way down, he turns. 'Well, in case you get there, I'll look out for you.'

Heilsburg

Mam's so excited anyone would think she'd a wedding to go to. She's washed her best and second-best outfits and as we sit down to breakfast she's ironing them dry at the far end of the table. She wants to try them both before deciding which to wear. Dad's in the doorway, about to leave for his Saturday half-day.

'I might not make it back in time to change, love. But that don't matter, do it?'

Pointing the iron into a ruffled hem, Mam doesn't see my dad wink at me.

'Come in or go out, there's a cold wind blowing,' she says. 'And if you think you're taking me dancing in your work clothes, Davey Quirk, you've another think coming! You'll wear a shirt and tie and your good black jacket, or we shan't go at all.'

'That old thing.' He means the jacket from his wedding suit. 'I was skinny as a rake then from the rations. It would barely go round me now.'

'Da-vey!' Mam warns, but she is smiling now because she knows he doesn't mean it. Dad kisses her on the cheek, and bangs the door behind him.

The war memorial hall was to open before Christmas but building works ran late, so now we've another shot at the party season. A week of celebrations starts today. I ask Mam isn't it odd to hold a dance to remember the dead? Like dancing on a grave. She sighs and tells me I'm too old for my years — something she says a lot when she's not telling me I'm too young for this, that or the other thing. She says if I must know, the war was party-party-party start to finish. 'When food and drink were scarce there was always dancing.'

I gaze at her, convinced she remembers it wrong.

'Folk had to keep their spirits up. For all they knew, each night could be their last.'

Mam looks sad, and I know then who she's thinking of. Once when I borrowed an old handbag of hers for a game I was playing, his photo fell out: too young for his Air Force jacket, like a boy scout playing dress-up, and next to him she was small and pretty and proud.

'Mam, can I go? There's child tickets for one and six.'

'No, Gwynn. Anyway, haven't you revision to do?'

'Jessica Brown's going.'

Jessica's mum sings with the brass band, and she's to go on stage and hand her a bouquet. I don't tell Mam there's a boy from my class in school going; it would only make things worse. There's no rush, she'll say, any time now. The world won't go away just because you've an exam, it'll still be there next time you look.

'No love, I'm sorry. I need you here to take care of your brothers.'

'But Ma-am, Mrs Reeves will be here. She'll look after them. Oh please?'

Mrs Reeves from across the field is all right, I suppose, but you have to tell her everything three times because she doesn't use her hearing aid.

Mam stops ironing and frowns, considering. This makes it all the worse when she tweaks my chin to make me smile and says, 'Sugar, if you came, Archie would want to come too. You and Archie's one thing, but say if Little Davey woke up? Mrs Reeves might not hear him.'

I glare at her, eyes wide to hold in the tears.

'Next time, Gwynn. Next time you'll go, I promise.'

What next time? Next time they build a village hall? Next time there's a grand opening dance? She might as well be the Queen Mother telling Princess Margaret, 'Never mind all that fuss over the coronation, dear. Next time, you'll be queen.'

Kamerwyk

Mrs Reeves arrives at six thirty. Mam has the table set for tea and excuses herself to get dressed. We lift the upside-down plates; underneath are jam sandwiches, slices of leftover fruitcake and buttered Rich Tea biscuits. As we finish eating, Mam and Dad stand in the kitchen doorway looking just like their honeymoon photo: him in the dark suit, her in a baby blue dress and fake pearls. She smells of 'Lily of the Valley' and looks like a queen. We laugh when she knots a scarf over her hair and pulls on her galoshes. Takes the shine off their outfits, but it's windy as anything now, and raining hard. Perfume kisses from Mam, stern warnings to behave from Dad, and they're gone.

I do the washing up like I've been told, but that's it. I will not sit by the fire, tuning the wireless for Mrs Reeves. Not tonight. Instead I go to my loft room. When I turned eleven, Dad cut a window in the ceiling and made a wooden stair, steep as a ladder, so's I wouldn't need to share a bedroom with my brothers. If I grow any taller I'll have to hunch over to get in, but it's mine.

Downstairs, Mrs Reeves has the volume cranked so high that the *Light Programme* bubbles insistently through the floorboards. Pulling the eiderdown round me, I stand by the window looking at where the sea would be if this was a proper island. Maybe Johnny Deakin's right, maybe there is a moon, but I can't see it yet, although the sky is light enough to make out the Downs on the mainland where Hadleigh Castle stands. I sink onto the bed, curl up fully dressed. What did he mean exactly — he'd look out for me? I picture his brown eyes and his bright smile and I don't care what Mr Frome says, I think Johnny Deakin's clever in a way. It's just maybe his way is different.

Komberg

When I wake the wind's tearing at the trees as if to rip them out by the roots, but all I care about is whether it's too late to sneak out to the dance. I slip downstairs past Mrs Reeves. Instead of getting into the folding bed, she has fallen asleep by the fire to the hiss of the detuned wireless. A quick check of my parents' room confirms they are not yet back. I grab my coat and am running along Brandenburg to the creek by the time I wish for my gloves and scarf. It's not just raining, it's snowing: long sharp needles of it pointing into my skin.

I've never been out in a winter storm at night, but the last thing I feel right now is fear. More, exhilaration. A bizarre conviction that if I can find the right place for take-off, I'll be able to fly. Near the high street I'm suddenly cautious, but when I peek at the hall from round a street corner, there's no sign of my parents. Just a few musicians loading their instruments into a van, an old man pottering about bolting doors and switching off lights. The sleet must have seen the crowd off quick. As for my parents, I guess they're at Dot and Arthur's.

Making an about-face I find the wind against me, pushing like it wants me to fall over. As I pass the creek on my way back I can't resist climbing up. The water's just off the top of the sea wall. Waves slap against it viciously, sending up cold drops of spray that hit me full in the face, but even now I feel no fear. Not while I'm here in the path of the gale and the waves. That comes later: when I've raced downhill and can see the white spray arcing over the wall, high above my head.

A sudden 'what if?' A logical question: what if the banks holding back the sea gave way? Yesterday the water would have tipped my brother's head. In this freak high tide, it might reach the rooftops of the bungalows dotted about the island. Ours is on a grass road in the Sunken Marsh, sea walls on three sides of it. From a place outside myself, I see the island like a huge sandcastle poised in front of the waves, ready to crumble.

The sudden fear speeds me onward, but when I reach home all is as before. All right, so it's windy, it's snowing even, but nothing worse. Not yet, anyway. I check the ground floor rooms. My parents still out, my brothers sound asleep.

Little Davey I lift from his cot. I hover by the steep wooden steps, afraid to drop him, until Mrs Reeves wakes and asks what I'm doing. She takes him from me as if to help. I clamber up the ladder, lie on the floor of my room and hold out my arms for him.

But she has moved away. She tells Davey, 'Big Sis is making a fuss over nothing,' as she carries him to her armchair. 'Old Hitler couldn't get me off this island. Blowed if I'll panic now over a drop of rain.'

I dart back to the boys' room for Archie. With some trouble I wake him and push him up to the loft, shuffling his sleepy body ahead of me on the steep wooden steps.

'Where's Mam and Dad? What's happening?'

'Don't worry. They'll be back soon.'

At the window I watch and listen a moment. No lights in the houses nearby, no signs of activity. Maybe Mrs Reeves is right, and it is just another storm.

But then a strange unidentifiable rumble makes itself heard above the wind. For a moment I stand and stare. Vibrations come up through the floor, and I hear rather than see the dark mass of water curl thunderously inland. The first sign of its progress is a curved white object hurtling toward the house: a caravan borne clear of hedges and garden walls by the massive wave.

Sskkrrrkkkss. Downstairs a window shatters. Seawater gushes in as if trying to flush us out of existence.

I race for the ladder to go for Davey. Archie follows. I jump back up, push him against my bed.

'Stay there, Arch.'

My foot touches icy water. I yell at him, 'If water comes up here, climb out the window on to the roof.'

Downstairs the water's up to my thighs and rising fast. The lights are out but I'd know my way blindfold. I feel for Mrs Reeves' armchair. Gone. Something hits my leg: there's furniture floating about the room.

Somewhere close by, Mrs Reeves is screaming. The front door opens and for a second I see her in the moonlight, holding little Davey. Then they are sucked out into the surge of water charging along the dyke.

A tow drags me after them and all I'm thinking is I must grab Davey from her in case she lets go. What stops me is this: my mother's oversized oak sideboard slams into the doorframe and blocks it. I crash against it, and something hits my head.

Landsburg

I wake choking on salt water. It's up over the picture rail now. I think it's my head bobbing against the ceiling that rouses me. My arms and legs are so cold it's an effort to move. I thrash around, colliding with floating chairs, until I find the steps and haul myself into the loft. Archie and I hold each other a long time.

Incredibly, up here in my room nothing is wet. This makes me laugh hysterically. I pull off my wet clothes and change into dry ones, numb and clumsy with shock.

Everything happens in slow motion now.

Out back, bits of garden shed are tossed on the waters like matchwood. We see no people, but we hear them. The screams of people who've not made it to safety. Like the shrill sound Mrs Reeves made. That is the worst thing. Sitting there, useless, listening to the screams.

Newlands

I've pushed the window wide open and am sitting on the ledge, feet on the bed. Archie is curled on my lap, his small warm body the last normal thing left. Water licks gently at the bed, sending the covers adrift.

Earlier, for a time, we heard the ferocious roar of water, the slam of objects against each other, a helpless bleating of animals and humans. Two voices sang as the water crept higher: nearer my god to thee. The belated wail of a siren. And fireworks too, that weren't really fireworks of course, nor even flares, but power lines pulled taut, exploding in a flash of orange sparks. But for an hour now while we've waited for dawn, there've been no more voices. No more shouts, no splashes.

'Why is it so quiet?' Archie asks, and I say people are resting. Saving their energy.

If it goes any higher we'll climb on to the roof and shout for help. In the end, though, it is their shouts that reach us.

'Hullo-o, hullo-o? Anyone the-ere?' The glimmer of a hand-held torch slips between islands that are the rooftops of flooded homes. 'Anyone the-ere? We have a bo-oat.'

'Over here!'

A shadowy boat approaches. A fishing boat. A skinny man leans forward and grabs the window to hold it steady. We scramble aboard, first Archie, then me.

'Gwynn?' the skinny man says.

Johnny Deakin.

I don't say his name, or thank you, or anything. What is there to say?

He gives a quick almost hug as he wraps a blanket round me and my brother, then nudges us toward the cabin. He goes back to shining his torch off the front and calling out. It's the older man steering the boat, who asks, 'Were your parents at home?'

I shake my head. 'Out.'

'Anyone else?'

I'm silent. Too many ifs swirling round in my head: if I'd fetched Archie quicker, if I'd not listened to Mrs Reeves, if I'd only held Little Davey tight.

The man makes a low whistle. 'Would you believe it: them gas lamps are lighting still.'

I can't believe he has room in his head to notice this, but I follow his gaze and he's right. A line of greenish streetlights glows eerily beneath the sea. The man uses their light to steer an obstacle free course towards higher land. Under the scratchy blanket I feel a patch of warmth where Archie's head rests against my arm, and I lift the blanket so it covers my face. I just want to go home. I want it to be yesterday, and none of this to have happened.

Nordland

In the morning two army lorries come for us. A soldier swings me up in back. At one end some half-dressed people are piled together, staring at me with eyes that have seen every bad thing that happened in the night. I sit Archie with his back to them so he won't see their frightened eyes. The soldier throws a blanket over them and tells us they're sleeping, but I know he's lying.

The wheels of the lorry churn muddy wavelets as we edge across the waterlogged bridge to the mainland. When we reach dry land I stare at the road ahead, unable to believe how normal everything is here; no mud, no water, no chaos. We pull up outside the new school in Benfleet and follow the soldiers into the assembly hall. Inside, it's all rigged up like a jumble sale without the bunting or the toffee apples. Ladies bustle about carrying bundles of clothes and blankets, and food that looks like party food, but isn't. They set it on two rows of desks, and a kind lady with white hair and a flowery dress asks would we like breakfast. I'm not hungry, but Archie eats cold soft toast with jam before running off to play.

All day the lorries bring people. I sit for hours by the double doors checking every new face, but none belongs to Mam or Dad.

Archie has been running with a gang of small ones as if they're at an extra-long birthday party. In the afternoon a man comes to claim his kids. Everyone smiles when he twirls the toddlers in his arms, but when his friends have gone Archie starts to cry and says, 'It's not fair. I want to go home too.'

'We can't. We have to stay here.'

'When will my Mam and Dad come for us?' he asks over and over. 'Where are they?'

I tell him they'll come tomorrow.

While he and the small ones are having supper I hear the women talking about whether Canvey can be rebuilt, or whether we'll have to shift to the mainland. On parts of the island where the waters aren't so high, they say, people have refused to leave. I try to think what I want. I would go back, I think, but only if everything's like it was before. Little Davey, too.

Strasbourg

After supper the small ones curl up on PE mats at the back of the hall, while at the top end the women huddle round a sputtering wireless to hear the news. Numbers ebb and flow: how strong the wind, how high the waves, how many dead this town, how many that. 'Dozens are still missing from Canvey Island,' the tinny voice says. When it stops, the women swap their own stories.

'It weren't our boat, it just sailed into the garden — Johnny got ahold of it and tied it to the chimney with a length of hose. We broke the bathroom window and climbed on to the roof, and there it was. Soon's we was on dry land, off they went, him and his dad, rescuing folk . . .'

'The Leigh fishermen came for us in their cutters. If it weren't for them . . .'

'It was Lars picked us up, the Dutch fellow, you know, that lives on a houseboat? Seven of us he had on his little rowing boat.'

I shuffle to the dark part of the hall where the little ones are sleeping, and curl myself round Archie who smells of dirt and sugar and think, What if? What if the sea walls gave way as Mam and Dad were walking home? What if they're alive somewhere in another shelter? I ache to see them, yet I dread it too, for I didn't do as I was told. I didn't take care of Little Davey.

Waalwyk

Night-time and I wake to the low grumble of men back from the island. The tide's in, nothing can be done till daylight. The white-haired lady sets a mug of cocoa in front of me and says she'll see me tomorrow. Her way of telling me no one came for us while I was sleeping. I don't want to sit with the grown-ups so I stand alone, watching the yellowy light of a torch pick its way through the hall, two or three shadowy figures following behind all jumbled together like an octopus.

'What will you do, Gwynnie?'

I know this voice before I look.

Johnny Deakin. His face is in darkness but he's right next to me, so close I could touch him, his hair spiked up with wind and salt water.

'Don't know. And you?'

He pulls a hand through his fringe as if to flatten it, but it stays standing. Behind him the octopus reaches the PE mats and slows. A couple, probably, seeking a space to lay a sleepy child.

'Mum says we're to go to her sister in Hastings. She's leaving tomorrow. Me and Dad will stay another day to help with the rescue if the soldiers want us.'

He sounds calm. Grown-up. Why am I such a baby? Why do I pretend things can still be the same when I know they can't? I watch the torchlight dance over the sleeping children, never resting more than a second so as not to wake them.

'What about your house?' I ask.

'Rented. We'll rent another. Mum says we've nothing to go back to here.'

I stare into my empty mug, not wanting him to see me cry. My hair falls over my face and he lifts a strand of it and tucks it behind my ear.

'If it was down to me . . .' Johnny Deakin says. 'But . . . You could come visit some day? Or you could write, if you can read my spelling.'

He hands me a torn page with an address on it.

I smile and make a fist over the scrap of paper, his hand warm on mine. I feel his breath on my cheek, the blood in my ears suddenly loud enough to hear.

The torch beam comes to rest on Archie. A gasp, and a figure detaches itself from the octopus and moves towards him, then gently lifts him up. Archie stays asleep, his head cradled on the man's shoulder. I step forward so as to ask what this man thinks he's doing, and my hand falls open as I realise it's them.

'Gwynnie?' a voice is calling. 'Gwynn. You here?'

I run.

In a second I'm in her arms, heaving with strange stupid sounds that are not even words, and her arms are warm around me, and I don't have to tell her about Little Davey because she knows, I know she knows.

Freshwater Habitat

He calls her as soon as the London markets close. It's been a jittery Friday, the futures markets all over the place, but Conleth never lets market emotion get to him. His own fluctuations today have been linked to another factor: to Aoi, who has been out of contact all day.

'So, did you get my email?'

'What email?'

'About Seán's wedding. I texted you as well.'

'Nope. I went shopping after work, I only just got in. The wedding's next month, isn't it?'

A pause.

'Isn't it?'

Conleth holds back from saying: 'Why do you even carry an iPhone?' because he's given up on expecting Aoi to be geeky on account of being Japanese. Besides, he never reproaches a girl-friend: it's one of his key strategies for dealing with beautiful women. And all his girlfriends without exception are beautiful, though he rates himself as severely challenged in the looks department. A tall thin body is one thing, but a tall thin face is something he works hard to mitigate, offsetting it with his mellifluous voice.

And so Conleth simply says, in the calm reassuring tones he

reserves for meetings with jittery clients, 'The wedding's tomorrow, but not to worry. Just chuck a few things in a bag and grab a
taxi to City Airport. I'm going straight from work so I'll be there
ahead of you. Can you make it by sixish, would you say?'

At Dublin Airport they hire a car. The journey is shorter now
thanks to the new road – the motorway there were all those
demos over because it goes past the Hill of Tara. The new road
doesn't quite reach Navan yet but it will do soon, and with his
valuer's eye Conleth knows that if he wants to buy property in his
home town, now is the moment to do so.

They turn off at a pub called Tara-na-Rí, and are soon enjoying the opulence of their hotel. It was Seán who tipped them off
about this place; a country house Conleth had never even heard
of growing up in Navan. The long tree-lined driveway was built
for horses and carriages, and the main house boasts a sweeping
staircase, up which a previous owner is said to have charged his
steed, leaving it trapped for weeks in the attic.

When the Anglo-Irish gentry ran out of cash in the years
following Irish independence, houses like this were either burned
or left to rot, unless of course they were taken over by the church.
Whatever fate it suffered then, this particular house is now in
full swing once more, its present incarnation one of the many
changes that have percolated across Ireland in Conleth's absence.
Staying here is not cheap but their vast room, with its ornate
ceiling and tall Palladian windows, feels worth every eurocent.
Last night Aoi said staying here makes her feel like the star of
a big-budget movie. Right now she is adrift in an ocean of
crumpled linen looking quite the sleeping goddess. So far, it's
been a pretty good movie.

But as he rubs himself dry after his shower Conleth notices that the room temperature is uneven; it's icy by the tall windows. Such failings bother him. He'd happily stay in a Marriott if there was one. A Marriott, in Navan? He smiles. Eight years ago this was unthinkable, but now that coachloads of tourists can rock up to the Hill of Tara on the new motorway, anything is possible. If townhouse apartments and gourmet restaurants are flourishing, why the hell not a major hotel?

He makes a dash for the bed, jumping under the covers instead of dressing for breakfast like he'd planned.

'There's a frost thick as snow outside,' he tells Aoi. 'Gives the jacuzzi a bit of a Finnish vibe.'

'I might skip it then,' she says sleepily.

'Ah c'mon. You'll be kicking yourself if you don't give it a go. It looks amazing.'

'Room service is amazing too. I'll stay in bed, you go.'

Conleth rests his icy skin against her warmth and she squeals in protest, yet does not pull away.

There's something about an indecently expensive hotel that invites women to behave with abandon, he thinks. A selling point which never quite gets a mention on the room reservations page but is worth factoring into the equation, all the same.

While the speech before his own drags on, Conleth observes the other wedding guests. Guys he once played hurling with, guys he sat next to in Chemistry or Irish, their faces redder and tougher now, leathered over. When they collected their exam results and went their separate ways it seemed, with his university place, as if he was on a winning streak, but now he's less sure. These guys aren't losers, they're just getting on with life, enjoying it. They don't have hard-to-please exotic girlfriends; they've married women with accents like their own who reliably furnish them with hot dinners and babies and satisfied little pot bellies. And if they throw short wishful glances at Aoi, well, he envies them too: living all year round in the halo of these wide horizons instead of spending one month in three flying business class, chasing deals.

Conleth wrote his speech at the airport, typed it up on the plane, and got the hotel receptionist to make him a print-out. He hasn't had time to learn it off so he reads it out as best he can, hoping it's up to scratch. Finally it's over. Seán gives him a short mannish hug and disappears on his rounds of meet-and-greet, leaving him to play catchup with the lads from the hurling team. He glances over at the women, posed for a group photograph, and hopes Aoi will cope with the girl bonding thing.

'Grand speech there, Conleth. You did Seán proud.'

'You always used to run rings around the rest of us with words.'

'Didn't old O'Shea once swear you'd be a poet? That your line of work now, Con?'

'No. Still in the financial sector, still looking for an exit strategy. It's less sexy than poetry, but it pays the bills. And yourself?'

'Running the farm. The brothers have found better things to do up in Dublin. Orla looks after school visits and a B&B, so we're mad busy in the summer. Lovely and quiet now, but.'

'That's what I miss. The fishing, and the quiet. Catching wild brown trout on the Blackwater or the Boyne. You can't beat it.'

'If you're around in the week I'll lend you a rod and a few of us'll go out?'

'Love to, John Joe, but I'm due back in work on Monday, placing bets how much things will be worth six months from now. Fun, huh?'

'Well if you change your mind, you know where to find us.'

Curled on the chaise longue in the hotel drawing room the next morning, headphones in, Aoi flicks through a copy of *Image*, a fashion magazine filled with models who are the progeny of Dublin footballers, barristers and pop stars. Conleth wonders what she makes of it, but doesn't ask.

It's a plus point that he never knows what she is thinking. His previous relationships were often painfully low on mystery. The women who go for him see him as safe-bet material, but he has never felt the same way. Except with Louisa. He was convinced they were made for each other, and they did stay together three years. Three years in which she insisted she would never settle down or have children, only to elope with a man from his work. She lives in Sussex now. He never hears from her, but the husband is still with the firm and has taken paternity leave. Twice.

Aoi drops the magazine, jumps up lightly and stretches.

'So, we're not visiting your mother again, and there's no more wedding stuff on . . . Shall we go out?'

'Might as well. There's a few places I want to show you, and we'll find lunch somewhere along the way.'

A fresh frost has landed on top of yesterday's, leaving the ground so white it's like snow. Conleth struggles on the uphill stretches of the small road, the car rolling backwards from time to time, careening towards the ditch. He wills the engine to respond before a collision with a stone wall triggers an excess fee.

First stop is the Hill of Tara.

'It's not a huge drop, mind, more of a slow burn slope,' he tells Aoi as they get out of the car. Having brought girlfriends here before, he knows he has to manage their expectations. 'And for a palace, it's all a bit sort of low key and organic.'

'Don't spoil it Conleth. Let me see for myself.'

They're in the churchyard, aiming for the side gate. The entrance is surprisingly light on official signage. Perhaps the government, embarrassed by the modest scale of this ancient seat of the Irish kings, chooses not to draw attention to it. Or perhaps it's played down because of the Daniel O'Connell connection, and because the border with Northern Ireland is not so very far away. A diplomacy thing. Who can say?

Aoi scans the hillside uncertainly. This could be any bit of pastureland but for the grassy circles with their stone doorways underground. She skips over the frosty grass and up one of the mounds.

To Conleth this suddenly feels very science fiction, like they could enter another world this second, if they were only to stand in the right spot. He tries and fails to remember how many counties you're meant to be able to see from here. He cannot see the motorway, cannot hear a single car. All that protest, for what? Won't more people come and see Tara now? Isn't that a plus? Or would the protesters have rathered keep the place to themselves?

Up by the Fáil Stone he takes a series of photos, turning on the spot after each click until he's made a full circle. Later he will run the images through an app that joins them in a single panorama, and will find that the image contains multiple Aois darting about from one ring fort to the next.

Next stop is the field. It lies on a slope between Tara and the town, high up enough that the view is still good. It's three years since Conleth has been here. The gate is rusted solid and he clambers over it like a trespasser, for the latch won't open. The grass has become long and straggly, and weeds have taken hold around the edges. Two adjoining fields are on sale now, he notices, which kind of opens up the options a little.

'What's this? Another place of ancient kings?'

'A kingdom yet to be built.' He grins. 'Just some land I bought once in case I ever move home.'

'Home?'

'Back to Navan.' He'd planned one time to make the old stone barn into a summerhouse for himself and Louisa, add extra rooms when they had children. Once she left, he lost interest in the project. Until now.

'You'd give up London, for here?'

She sounds concerned. Aoi worships London.

'I could go freshwater fishing whenever I wanted.'

But Aoi doesn't eat fish — a fact she claims was a huge liability growing up in Hokkaido — so she remains unimpressed.

'And for work?'

'I'm thinking of building a hotel. A really plush one.'

She slips over the gate. 'Sounds expensive.'

'A client of mine has a Marriott franchise in Spain. If you bring them a perfect site, they invest. Perfect means it's got scope to whack in a golf course and spa.'

'Golf? But why? What's special about this place is, it's so empty. And for miles around, people leave it that way.'

'If it's special more people should be allowed enjoy it.'

'Plonk a hotel here, a golf course there, and it won't be special any more. Why would you do that?'

Conleth smiles.

'I could retire tomorrow if I pulled off a deal like that.'

'Your kind never does retire.'

Her quiet, matter-of-fact voice bothers him. What does she

know? He is the one who makes predictions for a living, not her.

'And what kind is that?'

'Deal fixers. They're addicts, making the same thing over and over. It's different in London, rubbing out one building and putting another in its place. But here? This place is so . . . open. Why trash it?'

She walks towards the car.

Conleth chose a late check-out when he booked the hotel, thinking they might go back to bed on Sunday before they leave. He doesn't do a thing now to rescue that possibility, though he can feel it slipping away. Neither of them wants lunch, so they go to a tea room in a cottage near Tara. Aoi buys postcards of the Stone of Destiny.

'It's not as though it's what I want,' Conleth tells her. 'To me golf is a necessary evil, a game I play a few times a year when I've to entertain clients.'

Aoi is writing postcards. Her head is bent, her fringe fallen over her face, so that when he looks for her eyes all he sees is the strand of hair she dyed blue. Her name means Blue, too. It's the one word of Japanese he knows how to write. 碧.

'Golf is part of the franchise package, Aoi, that's all. And a good franchise makes the difference between a risky hotel venture, and a license to print money.'

'Is it?' She looks up briefly between finishing one postcard and starting the next.

He examines the finished postcard, trying to read what she has written, only of course it's in Japanese. Maybe she has told her friends about the Irish kings who were crowned here long ago, how the destiny stone roared when a true king was chosen. Or perhaps she simply told them that she has had enough of Europe, that she is ready to return to Japan.

'You must see it's a great location,' he says. 'Guests will have Newgrange and Tara within striking distance. History and activities. Cross-market appeal.'

'You sound so old-school, Conleth. Like a salaryman.' She sets down her pen. 'Did no one tell you — the old formulas have stopped working. Listen to yourself, not to "the market". Why bring in coachloads of tourists, pollute the river? Why not make something more modest for people who enjoy fishing?'

The lady selling cakes is looking over. Would you ever hush up, he wills Aoi. This is no place to talk business.

'Good point, I'll think it over,' he says, to quiet her.

'There should be nothing but park around Tara.'

'Not a lot I can do about that.'

'In Japan it would be a national park.'

They sit in silence until the tea goes cold and her postcards are done. On the way out they stop to buy stamps.

'Excuse my looking across at you,' the lady behind the counter says, 'only I used to be a teacher at the national school. Your face looks familiar. Conleth, is it?'

He has no idea who she is, but says 'Yes. Conleth Bagnall.'

'Ah, I remember you well. Always top of the class in arithmetic.' She hands him a euro in change. 'So Conleth, have you plans to come back to us?'

'I'm only over for a friend's wedding.'

He turns the coin over in his palm: on one side is the harp that was on the money he bought sweets with as a child; the fish that swam on the back has disappeared. Last year, on a fishing trip to Iceland, he saw fishes on every coin. The currency was baselined to a fish: in the old days when they ran out of metal, dried saltfish would change hands instead of coins at the Reykjavik markets.

'Funny you should ask, though. Conleth is thinking of moving back here to start a business.'

The lady from the shop raises her eyebrows.

'Well, I've been mulling over some options, seeing if I can balance out the money side.'

'Isn't that always the hard part? I hope it works out for you, and that we'll be seeing you both again soon.'

'Thanks. I hope so too.'

Aoi sounds as if she means it, which surprises Conleth because all day he's been getting the feeling she's about to vanish from his life. But maybe he's wrong. He might need to revise a few expectations if he's to convince her to stick around, he might need to — what's that thing he's always telling his clients — 'adapt to survive'. But he's in with a chance. The shiny new coins jangle in his pocket as he follows her outside.

Neap Tide

All day long Panos was full of talk: how big the ferry was and how fast it went. Not like the rusty boats in Greece. Lisa thought the khaki sea looked wrong. So solid and soupy. When she fell for Panos, she had also fallen for his country — the endless sun, the golden siestas, the sparkly silver-blue Aegean. She wanted it all. And he wanted her just as he found her: the pale freckled skin that never took a tan, the bluey-green eyes that changed whenever he looked at them.

'You have the strangest eyes, little Lisa, my Lisaki,' he told her. 'Alien eyes. Like the woman who fell to earth.'

Had she been alone, Lisa would have killed time on the ferry by reading or by visiting the bar to chat up whoever grabbed her fancy. People on a sea crossing would tell you anything and everything about themselves, liberated by the fact you'd never meet again. She loved that, she loved the urgent necessity of cramming a life story into a single evening.

'*Ela*, tell me a story, Lisaki,' Panos said. 'Tell me a story from when you were little, to pass the time.'

Panos came from a world that respected talk. He himself could talk like an angel — this she knew, for he had talked her into skipping her return flight, talked her out of one life and into another. But right now Lisa itched to read a new book. In Athens as her fortnight's holiday stretched into months, she had read *Giovanni's Room* five times, unable to find an English language bookshop. Once Panos found it lying open on the kitchen table and stuffed it away in the saucepan cupboard. When she asked why, all he said was, 'I hate books, they are so messy.' He filled the apartment with his own kind of mess: a jukebox, a wooden pinball machine, a 1960s' drum-kit, a huge wireless radio that he coaxed back to life by replacing its ancient valves.

Now he jabbed her arm urgently,

'The woman at the coffee bar, Lisaki. Look!'

Lisa saw a woman maybe a year or two younger than herself, mousey hair pulled back in a tight ponytail, a bored expression on her face. She wondered if the woman disapproved of the complicated range of coffees she had to serve now that here, like elsewhere in Europe, was a place where people knew their lattes and espressos from their cappuccinos.

Panos waited, expectant.

'What about her?'

'It's amazing. She has the exact same eyes as you.'

Lisa borrowed her dad's car and they drove into Dublin for the day. They spent the morning looking at shops and buildings. Things were a similar shape to before but the surfaces were glossier, and the trees that once sprouted from the sides of build-ings had been uprooted. Lisa realised it was some years since she'd spent any time in Dublin and that while she'd been learning other cities she had started to forget her own.

They walked across the Ha'penny Bridge and under the stone arch that led to Temple Bar and the inside-out bank. Panos came to a halt beneath the Why-Go-Bald man. He stood, entranced, watching the neon hair vanish, then grow again; vanish, then grow again. Each time his hair grew back, the man smiled and his head was haloed with red neon rays of happiness. The sign had been there since before Lisa was born. Sadly for Dubliners with thinning hair, the miracle it advertised worked only on neon men. Lisa set the timer on her digital camera to photograph the two of them standing beneath the sign. The timing was off. She was aiming for a picture of the smiling man with hair, but all three photos it took were of his bald alter ego.

The clouds softened into a single grey mass and drizzled down on top of them, so they ducked into a nearby cafe.

Panos tousled her damp hair as if she were a puppy that he had in training, 'My little Lisaki, you are so sweet, you are so special to me . . .'

Tall stained glass windows refracted coloured light over their coffees and sugared buns, and Lisa felt odd being with him here, where at any moment Eithne or Conleth or Janey might stroll in and ask who he was. Only of course they all had jobs now. They weren't about to breeze into Bewley's on a wet weekday afternoon and call out, Liiisa, how's it goin?

'. . . the most precious little alien in all the world. But tell me, Lisaki, my sweet one, how is it all the other little Irish girls have eyes just like yours?'

She wanted to hurl the sugared buns in his face. Instead she plucked her new book from its Eason's bag, but could only read the same words over and over.

She left the table and went to the ladies, where she rinsed her eyes with cold water and looked in the mirror. Maybe Panos was right, maybe she was not so special after all. Not even alien special. Then she looked at the other women, gathered in front of the mirror to comb their long hair or redo their make-up. Brown or hazel, blue or grey: no two pairs of eyes were the same. What was wrong with him? Couldn't he see that?

In Athens, Panos was the one who drove them everywhere in his scruffy 1950s' convertible or, more often, on the Vespa. It made a change now to be up front choosing the road. Lisa didn't feel like going straight back to her parents' house so she passed the turnoff for the suburb where they lived and drove on, pointing the car at the rocky Portrane coast. Beside her Panos dozed, lulled to sleep by the car's motion.

The townhouse apartments next to the train station threw her. For a moment she thought she had taken a wrong turn, because in the Dublin she remembered Portrane had been far beyond the advancing acres of housing, but when she saw the old Martello tower she knew she was on the right track. And at the end of the winding coast road the strand was as wild as she remembered. She parked in the place where Dad always used to park. Without waiting for her passenger to get out of the car, she ran down the steps and along the shore to the rocks, ten years old again, eager to escape the taunts and squeals of her brothers, to hear only the waves as they crashed and rumbled through the rocks and caves.

Out here the tang of seaweed was strong, the ground jagged with shell fragments part way through their slow transmutation to grains of sand. Black and red rocks tumbled right to the water's edge saying *pliobarnach, pliobarnach* as the waves thundered through their crevices and blowholes. From the low grey rocks by the water's edge came the steady tap-tap of a boy collecting shellfish. One by one, he separated them from their rocky homes and dropped them in a bucket of salt water.

When they were little, her brother Cormac had once shown

Lisa how to do this. 'Pick one just above the waterline,' he told her. 'Don't just grab it. Tap on the shell first, then pull.' Sure enough the limpet relaxed its grip.

Cupped in her palm, shell side down, the pale orange flesh shone soft and wet and far too real. Lisa replaced the limpet on the patch of rock where she'd found it, but somehow it wouldn't stick. It didn't seem to know its own spot on the rock any more. Gently, she slid it into a pool, hoping the sea might find it a new home.

In spite of her pleas her brothers refused to tip their buckets in the sea when it came time to leave.

'I wanna show Mam,' Rory said.

Predictably, their mother displayed no interest other than to ban the creatures from the house. So her brothers counted up to see who had collected the most, then poured the contents of their buckets on the compost heap at the far end of the garden, where the smell of rotting shellfish would not reach the house.

Lisa turned away from the water and picked her way to the top of the beach, stepping over curly brackets of black seaweed that marked the tide line. In a narrow cove with rock formations to either side, she lay on the crunchy unfinished sand and hugged herself for warmth. A cloud opened briefly and a faint milky sunshine spilled out. She closed her eyes, imagining herself and Panos far away, on a different beach. In another climate.

The crunch of pebbles was audible moments before his voice. 'Lisa! Lisaki?' She kept her eyes shut.

'Are you hiding from me?'

This time the crunching sounds came from closer by.

He dropped on the sand next to her and she snuggled into

him, wanting a neon blaze of sunshine to arrive out of nowhere and bathe them in its warmth. Wanting to swap this cold and sludgy sea for the one she remembered.

Panos never said the thing about the eyes again. He didn't have to. Even while Lisa wished things would go back to the way they'd been before, she knew they could not. She would catch herself thinking, You're not so special to me anymore, either. You're just like my brothers, tap-tapping for a weak spot until you have me in the palm of your hand.

She returned with him once more to his country, to his sparkly silver-blue sea, but the tide had turned between them. She was just treading water awhile, catching her breath, waiting for the next big wave to take her on her way.

Fishtank

Sorcha cries a lot lately. Not about having a baby, that isn't real. She worries about whether she will get enormously fat and covered in stretch marks, and she cries over silly things like people skipping the queue in front of her at the supermarket. At four months, when she sees the sea of swirling blue dots, she has a rush of warm feeling towards the little video blob. Then the nurse presses the sensor into the cold gel on her belly, and the thing on screen tries to swim away. The picture zooms in on the head: a tiny skull in negative.

Sorcha says the face looks gruesome, and the nurse asks, 'Where's your maternal instinct?'

After that comes a guided tour of various body parts. Despite the assistance from the nurse Sorcha finds the images impossible to decode. To her they're just a blur of blue-white dots, a pulsing submarine shape. But when the nurse says, 'Look at his face' and 'See his tiny hands', she salvages a nugget from the conversation.

She thinks, Hey, so it's a boy.

When her friend Tania had twins Sorcha remembers thinking, she just would have baby boys. Tania never had any brothers, and she was always crazy about boys. At school, Tania was the first girl to smoke a cigarette and wear a bra. Later, she deflowered boys as a hobby. She had so many lovers before she got married that her husband used to cry when he thought about them. Now that she has twin sons holding her hands the whole time, he is jealous all over again.

Sorcha had wanted so much to be like her when they were both fifteen, but was scared to let it happen. So she is kind of shocked now, after the scan, to find herself finally becoming a bit like Tania, after all.

She is having a baby boy.

At her parents' house, the old photograph album is crammed with photographs of her big brother. Joey asleep in his carry-cot, Joey learning to crawl on a rug in the back garden, Joey with all the grown-ups gathered round adoringly.

'Where are my baby photos?' she asks.

'Look, you're in that one, aren't you? And that.'

Her mother points out bits of Sorcha behind or beside a two-year-old Joey, and goes back to her ironing. It seems to Sorcha as if they must have been saving on the cost of film by the time she came along.

'But don't you have any proper baby photos of me, like this?' She flips to the large print of Joey from before she was born, the one with the tracing paper over it to keep the colours from fading. In the photo Joey is dressed like a tiny man, but he has a head full of baby fluff.

'Oh, I don't know. Try looking in the garage.'

In the paint-spattered dresser where Sorcha's father hoards screwdrivers, pliers, nuts and bolts, one drawer is stuffed with paper folders filled with prints and negatives. But Sorcha still can't find her baby photos.

She finds images of herself and Joey as ghostly toddlers,

playing beneath black skies on eerie West Cork beaches. The faces are hard to make out in negative, muddy and underwater, like the baby's head in the scan. The prints are clearer but they are rare and lopsided. These are the left-behind pictures, the ones not good enough to have made it into the album or a wallet. In faded Instagram colours they show Sorcha obediently smiling for the camera, her hair neatly brushed, her dresses ironed. A serious, grown-up child. A child who is trying too hard to please. Meanwhile Joey, instinctively, pleases only himself: he runs away from the camera, bored, his hair blowing over his eyes.

Sorcha and TJ go on holiday somewhere hot and try to forget. They stay in an ochre town built on an estuary that empties into a warm, calm sea. Neither of them understands the language spoken here. They eat romantic dinners at riverside tavernas, and ask strangers to photograph the two of them like this is the last time they'll ever be together. Each night on the way back to the hotel, they stop on the bridge and watch the evening lights reflected in the soupy water.

TJ photographs Sorcha on the beach, her belly rounding out her swimsuit. She writes a postcard: *Dear Mum and Dad, having a lovely time. Weather great. By the way, baby due September.* She passes the card and the pen to TJ, who scribbles in the small gap that she has left, *TJ probable father.*

That night, TJ wakes up in a sweat. He turns on the bedside light and this wakes Sorcha too.

She asks if he's OK.

'I'm fine. Just had a dream about the baby, that's all.'

Taking this to mean he's getting used to the whole baby idea, Sorcha asks what happened in his dream.

'Somehow the baby got up on the roof,' he says, 'and I was scared it would try to fly down.'

'Why would it do a thing like that?'

'It's so stupid,' he says. 'It likes the idea of floating on air. I tried to rescue it, but I couldn't find a ladder.'

'So then what?' Sorcha asks.

He blinks at her. 'Well, that's when I woke up.'

Sorcha's not sure she believes him. She thinks maybe he's keeping something back. She asks,

'How did the baby get up there in the first place?'

'Oh I don't know, you left it there probably.'

The sea is dead glassy as the plane drops over the English coast. There's been a major heatwave in their absence, and the city streets are sticky as an ice lolly wrapper. The faces on the tube train look tired and grumpy from the heat, and Sorcha tastes the salt on her face before she even realises she is crying. She didn't mean to, she was only thinking how long it will be before she sees the sea again. As they unlock the door of their flat, the telephone rings. It's Sorcha's mother. She's had the postcard, and she wants to know when TJ and Sorcha will be getting married.

Finally Sorcha gets her off the phone.

'I knew I shouldn't have told her,' she says. 'At least I gave her a fake due date, so we'll have a few days' peace.'

'You what?'

TJ is theoretically on closer terms with his mother, who lives a very long way away. Australia, in fact. He sees her every five years, and they talk on the phone on Christmas Day. He tries to call her in the morning, around the time the family gets back from their picnic on the beach. If he calls in the evening, it will already be Boxing Day there. He hasn't told his mum about the baby yet.

Sorcha's mother rings back an hour or so later, sounding tearful. She's been thinking, with Joey taking so long to come out of his gay phase, perhaps a baby in the family isn't such bad news after all. At least she's looking forward to becoming a grandmother. Sorcha hands the phone to TJ and goes to bed.

'We'll have to get it a PlayStation before it hits school,' TJ says. Sorcha is not convinced he's thinking of the baby.

'Nice of you to take an interest, but I'm not sure a PlayStation's a good idea. Especially for a boy.'

'C'mon, you want it to be socially inept like all the other kids, don't you?' TJ asks. 'I mean, you know how important conformity is at that age.'

A conciliatory parcel wrapped in brown paper arrives from Ireland. In the parcel is a gift-wrapped package and a letter in familiar handwriting. *I expect you've got lots of baby things by now. When Joey was born I had enough for at least two babies.*

In fact they have bought nothing for the baby yet. It seems odd buying clothes for someone you've never met. What if they don't fit? In the parcel is a blue one-piece suit with a teddybear motif. Sorcha holds it up to her tummy. It's huge. The baby can't possibly be that big, she decides. How the hell would it get out? She puts it in a drawer and tries to think about something else. It's not even here yet, and already this baby's taking over her life.

I'm getting a haircut before the baby comes, she tells TJ the week of her due date. He asks why.

'It mightn't be practical wearing my hair this long.'

'Why not?'

'You know. The baby might pull it.'

TJ is watching a re-run of the *X Files*. He waits until an ad break comes up before saying, 'Look, if the baby pulls your hair you should tell it to fuck off and move out.'

She laughs. 'You can't do that to a baby.'

'Imagine what you'd do to me if I pulled your hair — why should it get special treatment?'

When Sorcha wakes up in hospital and looks in the fishtank, she is convinced the baby has been switched. 'It was meant to be a boy. They said when I had the scan.'

TJ yawns. 'Scans aren't definitive.'

'What do you know, TJ? That baby's nothing like us.'

'I should hope not — it's like something off *Star Trek*. Or *Doctor Who*. Anyhow, I was here while you were sleeping. Nobody switched it. We're stuck with this one, they don't do refunds.'

He scoops the baby out of the tank and passes it to her. The baby stares at them and wiggles its fingers.

Catching the Tap-Tap to Cayes de Jacmel

Lucien pulls at bits of broken wood near his sore leg, hoping to hear the hard rattle of plastic. He found two bags of crisps here before, and some sweets. But that was a long time ago now. Two, three days? He's been down here now, he doesn't know how long. How do you tell when there's no light and your phone battery is flat? Just inches away, there could be more food or drink that he hasn't yet found. Best keep searching. No use being all skin and bone when they finally pull him out of here.

Lucien wonders how many other buildings toppled in the quake. He wouldn't be surprised if this was the only one. The cinema was one of the older buildings in the neighbourhood, and it's not like his boss invested much in maintenance: on a windy day the place had always looked ready to fall down.

He hears a noise from off to his left. Tap-tap.

'You still hanging on there, Luc?'

The old woman, Agnes, her voice a hoarse whisper.

'Oh yes, I'm not going nowhere.'

Each of them is trapped in a separate air pocket. He's never seen Agnes, but since this thing happened Lu ien's got to know her voice. Agnes was watching a movie in the upper circle, so she must have dropped quite a way to be down here on the same level as him. Lucien was on the late shift, chalking next week's movies on the blackboard — a weekly task he liked better than his real job, which was selling cinema tickets and popcorn, and cleaning up after the show. At first he thought he'd knocked the board over, then he realised everything was shaking and falling.

'You've been quiet,' Agnes says. 'They've all been quiet awhile.' On day one she had told him she could hear five or six people tapping.

'They're resting,' he says. 'Keeping their strength up for when we get out of here.'

Agnes doesn't mention the ugly sweet smell that seeps in and mingles with the stale dusty air. Nor does he. Neither of them wants to think about that. Lucien knows he can't reach her, but to cheer her up he says:

'If I find more bon-bons, Agnes, I'll split 'em with you, I promise.'

'I'll hold you to that,' she says.

And he knows he's made her smile.

The smile in her voice reminds him of his mama. It's a long time since he spoke with her. Months now. Lucien misses her voice. When he was little, after his father left for Port-au-Prince, Mama would talk with him at night until he fell asleep. If he closes his eyes it's like there is no broken cinema on top of him. He's standing in the sunlight by Mama's house, breathing in fresh sea air. When this is done, if he gets out and walks away from this, he's going home . . . He stops himself.

Not if. When. *When* he gets out of here.

Mama's doing fine, he knows it. In the little village outside

Cayes de Jacmel where she lives, the buildings are small and light. Home is a single storey house. No concrete floors to fall and trap her. Besides, there's the timing: the quake came at the start of the evening shift. That time of day, Mama's always out and about feeding the hens. The worst that could have happened is she fell over and picked herself up again.

She's a strong woman, his mama. The night the hurricane blew the roof off, she made the children huddle together in the kitchen while the wind howled around them, little Rousseline crying and hanging on to her teddybear to keep it from blowing away. Before dawn, the wind calmed and they slept.

When they woke, Mama was gone. Soon, though, they heard her voice from outside: 'Luc, Zach, come quick and help me with this.' She had found the tin roof in some trees, and dragged it home single-handed. She battered the corrugated metal into shape and together they set it back on the walls, weighting it down with heavier stones than before. That's how strong Mama is.

Lucien finds no more chocolate, but in this darkness a glimpse of the outside world is better than any sweet. He feels stronger, the pain in his leg less sharp than before.

When this is over he's going to leave this damn ugly-beautiful city. It mesmerised him when he first arrived: the hustle like a hundred market days jammed together — too many people for him to know their names and remember their stories, like he did back home. But now he's been here a few months, Lucien knows that Port-au-Prince and Cité Soleil are not so special as they seemed from far away.

He also knows he won't be driving home in a 4x4 like he planned. That would have made Mama proud; she loves people to see how well her family is doing. But it would take years to buy a car like that, maybe more years than Mama has left. And she'll be pleased to see him as he is. That's good enough for him.

When Lucien told mama he was going to the city, she cussed him for two days solid. She barely spoke to him the day before he left, but the day he was to leave she got up before dawn, made him breakfast and watched him eat it. She even walked to the edge of Jacmel with him, though she rarely left the house so early except to tend to her animals. He didn't like to drag her up town at the crack of dawn, but he had to be there in good time in case the tap-tap left without him. If enough people came it would leave by seven thirty. If not, the driver would sit in his minibus smoking cigarettes until he sold enough seats to cover his petrol, then take to the road in the hope of adding a few more passengers along the way. That day Lucien was lucky. The tap-tap was nearly full, but not so full that he would have to stand on the runner outside, or sit up top.

All the way there, Mama hadn't spoken. Only after he paid and took his seat did she reach in through the air vent carved in the side of the bus, take his hand and say:

'I'm worried you'll be lost to us, Luc. I never once heard from your papa after he went to Cité Soleil.'

'I'm not like Papa. You won't get shut of me that easy.' He leaned out of the opening, kissed her, and handed her his phone. 'Look Mama, I need a new phone — you take this one. I'll call you tomorrow, OK?'

She smiled as the brightly coloured bus moved away.

The tap-tap climbed noisily up the steep hill that overlooked the caye, and Lucien felt dizzy when he glanced down a few minutes later. From up here you couldn't see their home — the whole village was hidden by greenery. Closer to town the long stretch of white sand was interrupted by fishermen's huts, a wooden jetty, boats. At the place on the edge of town where the sealed road made a loop and came back, a few buildings stood out: the market, the petrol station, the church. The crowd gathered at the bus stop had mostly scattered, but Mama was still there in her bright pink dress, waving her scarf.

He almost asked the driver to stop then and went back. But he didn't, he just leaned out and waved goodbye. He called her every night from Port-au-Prince until his old phone stopped working.

Lucien pictures himself telling his boss he has to quit. Then he grimaces, because after all, the cinema is lying in bits all around him. And who knows what's become of his boss? Even if he wanted his old job back, he can't have it.

Soon as he gets out of here, he's catching the tap-tap to Cayes de Jacmel. When he gets there, Mama will lay out a homecoming feast to celebrate, dishes ranged along the bench in the backyard: fresh fish cooked in banana leaves, rice, fruit . . . Everyone will be there, all their neighbours, old Ernesto with his guitar and a song, and his dazzling smile. It will be like a wedding without going to church. And he is going to dance.

Some hours later when Lucien wakes up, he is cold. His legs are stiff and the one that's been hurting feels like nothing at all. He taps the wall but no one answers, not even Agnes. For the first time he feels nervous. He remembers his grandma telling him how she saw the blinding white light that comes for people when their souls leave their bodies. Lucien was ten years old then, and was visiting Grandma in hospital. She fought the light off that first night, but it didn't leave so easy. Two nights later it came for her again, and this time it took her away. This is what he's thinking when the bright light comes for him.

Lucien shuts his eyes tight. He will not, he must not, see this light. The light of the dead people is not for him. He wants to live.

Tap-tap. 'You see it?'

Lucien shivers at Agnes's cracked whisper. He really thought she was gone this time. Maybe she belongs to the other place now, and has come to fetch him?

'See what?'

'You mean you don't see that light?'

The light on his closed eyelids glows red. He hears another voice. The words are muffled. Then, something about body heat and survival rates. Lucien smiles and opens his eyes. This is another light. The world is not ending, it's beginning again. Loud as he can, he shouts,

'Here, over here. We're here and we're alive.' And to Agnes he says: 'Do I see that light? Yes, I see it, and it's beautiful. What did we tell each other?'

Her voice is hoarse but bright with joy,

'*We* are getting out of here.'

Pole House

It's a hot January morning and Kate is alone at the Pole House. The twins rarely visit these days, and Thom is up the hill in his studio, working on his surf sculptures. Here in the bush hills behind Piha, she cannot hear the few cars that pass on the nearest road, only the distant roar of surf and the wind in the trees. The forest has flourished in the years since it was protected, and the only glimpse of the ocean now is where Thom has chiselled a gap with his chainsaw. Some days she follows the path through the bush to the sands, but today Kate needs to get away. Take a drive downtown, she decides as she rinses suds from her hair in the outside shower. Get a haircut, go see a film.

In a patch of morning sun she bends and flexes, making a circle with her arms each time she straightens. When she's done she pulls on jeans and sandals. Her stretches seem to work, for Kate has a girlish figure, though the lines scored on her face by the harsh Piha sun tell a different story.

As she's leaving she pulls out her phone and calls Thom. 'You feel like maybe taking the day off, coming downtown?' She's not expecting a yes, it's more a way of letting him know she has the car.

'I'm good here, thanks.'

'Can I bring you anything? Pastry from that new café? Maybe a new book?'

'Book? I've a massive deadline coming up.'

There's a frown in his voice, phone gripped between shoulder and ear so he doesn't have to down tools.

'Isn't the show in March?'

'I've five more surf pieces to finish. They need to ship weeks ahead to reach Amsterdam on time.'

It's amazing how many damn surf sculptures his agent shifts under the strap line 'bringing nature to urban homes'. You'd think people would want unique, but no, what they want is a failsafe investment: replicas of pieces already reviewed in glossy art magazines.

'Must be a drag doing repeats of the oldies.'

'I vary the medium, keeps it fresh. Clay, wood, rock, anything with a new break point. Besides, I'm never bored if I'm working, it's holidays bore the pants off me.'

Kate backs the jeep out fast and rear-ends a line of bubble-wrapped sculptures awaiting collection. One piece topples. When righting it she spies a dent that she swivels to the wall. She pulls away, giggling. Let it go all the way to Amsterdam — Thom's dealer will probably pass off the dent as intentional.

Joke really, Thom raking in all this money from surf. Back in the day, he was the one guy she knew who didn't go surfing. While the alpha males strutted their stuff, he would be making a bamboo shelter or whittling at a lump of driftwood. He would disappear off the beach into the bush for days at a time, barely missed. But she still remembers the day he showed her what he'd secretly made. Fashioned from branches, vines, bamboo, whatever came to hand, an elfin palace rose from the under-growth. On top was a sleep platform open to the skies where they spent a night and a day and most of another night before hunger drove them to the beach. Kate changed her mind about Thom then. He might be quiet and shy, but he not only planned up wild schemes, he created them. Lived them.

That hilltop bach, now his studio, is where they first lived together. The Pole House came later, set on a rocky slope near the spring. Her mother visited just the once. The dunny horrified her, and the rooms on stilts that creaked and swayed in tropical storms. Kate adored it. The full moon parties thrown here were legendary among a group of friends long scattered now. Their beach friends left for Asia around the time planning in Piha tightened up. That winter Kate saw the cluster of baches on the dunes pulled apart — the sight made her want to leave too, but Thom stood firm. Her friends flitted easily from one country to the next, sent the odd postcard asking her to join them, blamed Thom when she failed to show up.

Only when he won permission to stay, citing existing use, did Kate come to see Thom's love of routine as single-minded. Ambitious even. After those heady early days when life here was a flimsy game made up as they went along, the Pole House grew into a home. They raised children here, watched them leave. The pace of change is slow, the scenery still gorgeous, but to Kate the hard-won right to remain beneath this canopy of forest sometimes feels less of a freedom, more of a prison sentence.

For half a mile of rough dirt track the jeep is shackled at walking pace. Kate shakes her fringe out of her eyes; a mistake here could be nasty. She's had it with this. She wants to live close to other people, not an hour's drive from the nearest dairy. But Thom will never leave. This place is too much part of him.

At the end of the track she makes a right and speeds along a metal road that snakes through the hills. Sunlight slants through the foliage, picking out ferns and small palms. As she makes the bends, driving from shade into light and back again, the contrast makes her vision blink white and red. But Kate could drive this road blindfold and her pace never slows. Passing beneath the *Chance of a Fire Today* sign, she notes that for the first time this summer the needle has overshot orange and entered the red.

When she has left Titirangi behind and is on the motorway, Kate turns up the volume. It feels right to be out from under that shade, like she was on standby before and is now on full power.

As a student Kate would walk everywhere. She still likes to walk when she's out and about downtown; that way, she's free to change course without causing a traffic violation. She decides to skip the haircut in favour of a trawl through the op shops on Karangahape Road. A red light area in her youth, these days K Road is a student hangout. But there's no chance of bumping into the twins, they're on a field trip in Napier.

Kate checks out the cafes and bars, wondering which ones her boys go to, which she'd choose if she were a student. In one shop window a man with a Maori tattoo winds up clockwork toys. *Ray's Toy Shop*. He sees her looking and nods. Inside, they sell cakes, computers, coffee, toys, smoothies, fluffies, digital accessories, chocolate fish, teeshirts, coffee-makers, even music. I'd choose this place, she thinks, though I'm hardly target market. But before she can leave, the girls at the counter break off their banter to welcome her. While her coffee is being made, the guy with the tattoo goes by carrying a stack of DVDs. Kate takes a stool by the coffee machine, enjoying its volcanic eruptions of sound as she leafs through flyers for gigs she'll never see.

'Let me guess, you wouldn't mind an upgrade, but you're not in the mood to talk tech right now?'

Kate turns. It's the man with the tattoo.

'Cool if I sit here?' She nods and he says, 'Talking tech shouldn't be scary, eh, that's why I made the Toyshop an easy place to drop by.'

'I came in by chance. But as it goes I'd upgrade my laptop if I had a decent internet connection.'

'I'm Ray. To help you I'd need to run some diagnostics.'

'Fine, I guess.'

'It's just, the questions may seem a bit, well . . . I'm not being nosy, honest. Just need a bit of context.'

'OK.' Something about Ray makes him easy to trust. He looks not much older than the twins, though he must be older if he set this place up. He asks where she lives and Kate tells him.

'Amazing up there, eh?' he says. 'Right in the bush.'

'Mmm. Bit too remote at times.'

He grins.

'Nowhere's that remote any more, with the internet.'

'The connection up our way is prehistoric. Dial-up. When it's down, it's gone for days. Can you fix that?'

She's surprised by the speed with which he replies.

'Easy. Costs extra, but the cool thing is it works anywhere. Even the beach, if you want.'

'So tell me. What is it?'

'Satellite. Bounces the signal off a dish in the sky.'

His face is inches from hers, daring her on. She has a feeling Thom would disapprove, but Thom is not here. Maybe she won't even tell him. 'Can I have a demo?'

'Where's your laptop and I'll show you.'

'In my car.'

'My lunch break's just starting. Why don't we meet up at Mount Eden and I'll give you an on-site demo?'

So she's at Mount Eden on the high point where the crater once belched forth its stuff, facing the city and the dark volcanic sprawl of Rangitoto across the bay. And she's waiting for Ray to show up, feeling the way she used to feel: rushed, spontaneous, on edge. It's a weakness, she thinks, to need people this way. Thom has always been more self-sufficient. Her talent was for bringing people together, dancing round campfires and staying up till dawn. Later, making parties for the twins, she'd spend days painting fishes and seaweed, or castles and wizards. Once she hung rock friezes from the poles that support the house to make a cave. All that effort, for something remembered now only when an old photo opens a window into someone else's life. The photos reveal her supporting role to the reclusive artist, whereas at the time Kate thought herself an artist too, hoped she'd catch up.

'There you are! I was on the other side.'

'Oh, is the signal better there?'

Ray points at the sky. 'Signal's good everywhere.'

He sits on the grassy bank and holds out a hand for her laptop. He slots something the size of cigarette lighter in the USB port. It looks too small, too easy. He names a monthly fee but she's not listening; she's looking at his hair, oddly relieved to spy a strand of white behind his ear.

'We're in. So what do you want to download, lady?'

His ironic shop-boy voice makes her laugh.

'A map of the Desert Road.'

'OK, here you go.' In seconds the screen shows a map and photos of the flat state highway.

'That's pretty fast.'

'I like to come at Tongariro off Highway 47, myself.' Ray drags the map so the photos show green glacial lakes and a snowy hut, icicles blown sideways from its pitched roof. 'See? Perfect place to start the walk.'

'Walk? Don't you mean climb?' He is one of those people who make anything seem possible. Magic. Like Thom used to be. 'You win, Ray. I've got to have one.'

'And here I was hoping it would take a long lazy lunch to persuade you.'

She pays him cash and he sets the gizmo in her hand.

Then he slips the laptop in her backpack, and loops the straps over her shoulders like she's a child leaving for school. Kate shuts her eyes at his glancing touch, and sunlight licks her eyelids orange-red. *Chance of a Fire Today: High.* And now she can't see him any more, she can only feel. Warm skin on skin, lips that skim hers lightly: the sweet, easy perfection of that first touch.

Right now this heat, this surge of power, is enough, and for some moments she lets the light and the heat take over. It's a good feeling. Then Kate pictures dark smoke pouring from Rangitoto, lava-streams pushing down the walls of the last baches that still cling to its skirts.

Next time she does this she wants things to feel light all the way through. She pulls away and says, 'Race you downhill.'

Without waiting for a reply she starts running.

She runs hard.

Ahead of her Rangitoto bumps up and down with each stride. Kate can see the smoke pouring from its cone, steaming across the bay, can see the tremors rocking the Waiheke ferry. She keeps on running and the volcano sinks beneath a line of trees.

But Kate is no longer thinking about Rangitoto, or about anything, there's just the steady thud of her feet landing on the ground and the bag shifting on her back, and her breaths getting louder, then finally laughter as she flops on the grass and lies there watching a long white cloud pass over the bay.

Sound Waves

Shay loves the darkness when he arrives in the studio each morning, says he can hear better in the dark. His mum asks how he can stand to be locked away in the pitch black all summer. But it doesn't matter to Shay because he's doing what he loves. True, the money is rubbish. He's on the bottom rung, about on a level with a roadie, but when the last session of the day is done he has the chance to record his own songs. And he takes every chance he gets. Often, by the time he gets home, the dinner his mum cooked for him is shrivelled and the sun is long gone from the sky.

But the day he finds out about the festival, the sun is blindingly bright. Flying ants are swerving little waltzes in the air, on his shirt, on his arm, like he isn't even there. Shay swats them away and pulls out his mobile phone. It's his lunch break and he has been too busy all morning to answer it: humping gear, plugging instruments into amps, tracking the sound guy's every move so as to learn how to mix. Four new messages. He squints against the light to read the sender names. One from a club he's stopped going to, one each from Ellie and Matt.

Oh, and one from the festival. Himself, Ellie and Matt applied to work there because the tickets were sold out. It was Ellie's idea. She said if you did a few hours' work you'd get in free. They're still waiting to hear back.

An ant lands on the phone screen. Shay flicks it off and dodges into the corner shop. He fetches a cheese sandwich from the fridge and sets it on the counter. Then he reads the message: *Good news, you're in. You will work two shifts . . .* blah blah, he skips that bit, *and at all other times you will be free to enjoy the festival.* Perfect.

He sticks his card in the machine, ready to pay.

'There's a one-pound fee on transactions under a fiver,' the bloke behind the counter reminds him. Shay adds a drink and a few packs of chewing gum, pushing his bill up to £5.29. While the card is being processed he forwards the festival message to Ellie and Matt, adding, 'Yours come thru?' Then he opens their messages and sees they're asking him the same thing. Score!

On the way back to work he's not bothered by the ants or the plastic taste of his cheese sandwich: all he's thinking is what a cool time they'll have at the festival.

Livi is finding it hard to focus on the music. Last night she couldn't sleep. She went downstairs and munched half a dozen chocolate biscuits, and this morning her jeans wouldn't zip up. A bad start to the day, one that feeds her fears of being too old for this line of work. At thirty-seven, she feels older. Her teenage daughter thinks she's low on rock-star attitude, and has said so. Which doesn't help. But her daughter doesn't get the whole playing live thing. Never has, in spite of her gift for music. It's not up to you when you stop playing — not if you're in a band that the fans still want to hear. And thank Christ for small mercies, Livi thinks, at least I'm only on bass. Far worse to be up front under the spotlight, like Moro.

It's years since the Fa So La's toured or made a new album.

Herself and Moro turned down a few gigs recently but when the festival offered them a headline slot, their manager insisted. 'Look girls, it's not Glasto, but it's very influential,' he said. 'Yous are lucky to be asked. Just get a haircut, go on a diet maybe, and yous'll have a great time.'

Livi looks at her stomach, half hidden by the bass. She gains weight when she's stressed and has gone up a clothes size this past month. In contrast the session musicians who took over the vacant slots on drums and guitar are tall and thin in a retro, junkie sort of way. Next to them she's like a cartoon Jack Sprat's wife. The heat in the studio's getting to her, but the two Jack Sprats haven't a hair out of place between them.

Sweat makes her fingers slip on a key change. She stops playing and waits for the next in-point, but Moro cuts the song.

'Li-vee! What's with you? The run-through's for the benefit of the new guys, not the old hands.'

'Sorry.'

'Want to carry on?'

'Sure. Shall we go again from the chorus?'

'No, take it from the top.'

Moro counts them in again and Livi does her best not to feel belittled. Familiar chords start up: the opening bars of a song that made them a million back in the days when a million counted for something, and Livi finds that if she closes her eyes and stops worrying, her fingers know exactly where they need to be.

Ellie, Matt and himself leave for the festival early on the Thursday. The train is like any train, but when they board the boat to the island and are surrounded by other festival-goers, there's a real sense of anticipation. The sea is calm, the water flat.

Too flat almost, but then this is only a strait — the real sea is on the far side of the island. The wild side. As he watches the mainland recede, Shay has the feeling they are leaving reality behind. The festival is another world, a world of games and music and dressing up. A place where anything can happen.

They have backstage passes for the whole weekend and Livi is curious to hear the other bands, but Moro decides they're to keep away until the last minute. 'We need to be on form,' she says. 'Hanging around in a crowd could put us off our stride.'

On the Friday they do one last rehearsal. The whole set is pretty tight by now, those early disasters with timing all ironed out. Afterwards Livi and Moro go to a spa and get facials, a massage, new haircuts. Livi wonders how come she never noticed when they were starting out that so much of the music business is not about music at all.

'Got to look the part,' Moro says.

To Livi's relief she picks up the tab: royalties have been low this last couple of years, and Moro does earn the most, after all, because she co-wrote their hits.

Along with the two-man cowboy print teepee which all three of them have somehow squeezed into, Ellie brought tons of dried fruit, rice cakes, even fresh fruit. Matt's contribution is a backpack filled with vodka cocktails, siphoned into juice bottles to get them past security. All Shay packed was his guitar and a skimpy sleeping bag last used at scouts. It's late in the morning and Matt, Shay, and their camping neighbours are dozing in the sun on a small patch of grass between the tents, while Ellie tidies out the teepee. Watching her plump up the pillow on her sleeping bag, Shay smiles. Chalk and cheese, her and Matt.

Ellie shrugs as she comes outside. 'Had to bring it. Can never get to sleep without a pillow.'

'Sleep?' Matt says. 'That's the last thing that should be on your mind this weekend.'

The blokes from the next tent laugh. One of them taps the girl next to him who is stretched on a sleeping bag, sunning herself.

'Hear that, gorgeous? Think you're getting any beauty sleep this weekend? You're out of luck.'

The girl briefly lifts one of her pink headphones. 'I didn't catch that.' When the only response is laughter, she pops the phones back on and finger-dances in an infectious, good humoured way.

Matt grins and rolls on to his back. 'Brilliant. I'm telling you, this is gonna be the most brilliant weekend of your life.

Livi's been fasting all week, and has on a flattering pair of stretch jeans. There's a weird vibe backstage. A kind of invisible wall has grown up between the two session musicians, and herself and Moro. Added to this there's a whole separate war going on between Moro and the other headline act: a jostle for power over start times, set-ups, who has the most gear on stage, that sort of thing. Moro keeps telling anyone who'll listen that the other band are total divas. Livi tries not to get involved.

'Just going out for a few, get some air.'

Moro says, 'Don't be long.'

Shay tends to take Matt's predictions with a barrow-load of salt so he's surprised now to be thinking, Maybe Matt's right and this really is going to be the best weekend ever. They haven't had to work too hard: they did a session on the gates on Friday, taking tickets and fixing bracelets on the newbies. Last night he was up till three at a small outlying venue, the Chapel, jamming and partying and talking shop with other young musicians. It's late in the afternoon, the hiatus before the evening bands come on, and he's sitting on the grass outside the double-decker bus cafe, sunburned and grubby, strumming his guitar.

Every afternoon so far he has eaten at the bus cafe before going to catch the bands, but today he is broke so is making do with one of Matt's bottles of orange juice. Not the smartest way in the world to start the evening, he learns, as vodka scalds his throat.

He glances at the girl with the pink headphones, who has a job in the bus cafe. Late last night she turned up at the Chapel. Easily the high point of his entire festival. Only a handful of people were left on the dance-floor, dwindling to just the two of them for the last song. When the music ended they walked back to camp together and kissed, before zipping themselves into their separate tents. A big part of why he's so tired right now is because afterwards he couldn't stop thinking about her.

Today the girl's pink headphones dangle round her neck as she takes coffee orders. She shows no sign of having seen Shay arrive, but on her break she brings over two coffees and a flapjack and sits beside him.

'Hey. You look like you could use some sustenance.'

He bites into the flapjack. 'Cheers. Get you back later. You going up to the Chapel tonight?'

'Might do.' She shrugs. 'Got to eat a proper dinner at some point, or I'll be ill.'

Shay is surprised. She looks such a festival insider, and he's starting to believe Matt's theory that the only way to get through a festival is the marathon approach: put selected physical maintenance — sleeping, eating, and washing, for example — on hold until it's over.

'Don't they feed you here?'

'Sure, but my friend Julie who cooks at the Undersea Tavern has asked a few friends around tonight for a midnight feast. Sounds great — South Sea Soup, Seafaring Spaghetti, Shipwreck Pavlova with Salted Caramel.'

Shay looks away. Suddenly the attraction of the Chapel has palled. Not so much because of the food: he just wants to be wherever she is going to be.

Adrift in the crowd, Livi forgets her promise to return to the backstage area. Streams and eddies of people carry her over hills sloped like sine waves, dotted with marquees and small stages that each throw out a different sound. When she comes to the woods she follows a looping pathway between tall shadowy trees. In a clearing by the lake, thirty or so people are dancing around an outsized jukebox. But the music doesn't sound pre-recorded, and sure enough when Livi looks closer she sees half a dozen musicians crammed inside the jukebox, playing and singing live. They have an incredible range: disco, punk, ska, reggae, old, new, happy, sad.

Somehow hearing the jukebox musicians crank out rowdy, danceable versions of songs written decades ago gives her a fresh take on the Fa So La's. The sound of any individual band is just one drop in this tidal ebb and flow, this push and pull, this ocean of musics that makes one song popular this year, another the next.

So what if the Fa So La's scored a slot this year only because a younger, more fashionable band named their early hits as an influence? The fact they've been around awhile is nothing to be ashamed of. Music doesn't stand still, it is all about change. Right now their sound has floated up to the surface. Soon it will be drowned out again by other new sounds flowing into the mix. They may as well bask in the moment. Celebrate.

A text from Moro summons her backstage.

At the end of their set an exhausted Livi and Moro do the back-stage meet-and-greets, then make their way to the Undersea Tavern. The crowd loved them, and that's enough for Livi. Even Moro seems happy. As they move through the hordes they notice that the festival punters are wearing fancy dress tonight: jellyfish and sharks, umbrellas dangling octopus legs, swordfish, stingrays, sea urchins. On the grass outside the tavern a few young musicians are playing. The guitarist stops when he sees them, and comes over. 'Hi, I caught your set earlier. You were amazing.'

Moro says there's someone inside that she must catch up with. Livi smiles and thanks the young guitarist.

'Your whole sound really influenced me a lot when I was young,' he adds.

Livi tries not to laugh at the when-I-was-young bit, because he looks as if he's somewhere between the ages of sixteen and nineteen.

'It's still quite influential. To me, anyway,' she jokes.

He asks her about the lead guitar chords to one of their early hits, 'Saturday Night'. Livi isn't sure, but offers to play him the bass section to help work it out. Someone hands her a bass guitar and they start jamming.

When the girl with the pink headphones arrives, Shay doesn't notice at first because she's under one of those umbrellas with lights dangling from it. A jellyfish costume. He and the Fa So La's bassist are sitting cross-legged on the floor playing softly. They've nearly got the whole song, there's just one rogue chord they haven't managed to nail. When he sees the girl looking down at them, Shay thinks she's upset. He starts guiltily and stumbles to his feet. Looking at her clear skin, at the curve of her cheek, he's never been so alive, so completely in the now.

'Hey, I want you to meet Livi from the Fa So La's,' he says. 'This is . . .' And he feels stupid then, because he has never thought to ask her name. Whenever she is near, she is simply more there than anyone else, almost as if she doesn't need a name.

'. . . Carlita, my daughter!' Livi says, laughing. 'We're both here for the supper tonight. Will you be coming to that as well?'

'Uh, I don't think, I mean . . .'

'It sounds fab, all the food is sea-flavoured to match the dress-up thing.'

Shay feels awkward: he looks at the girl. Carlita. The name seems wrong for her, somehow. Too frilly.

'It's OK, we're all invited.' She whacks him lightly like they've known each other for years, not days. 'You too. I asked my friend Julie.'

In that second Shay knows he will be with this girl ten and

twenty years from now. He sees the slight curve of her nose in profile, and he knows that over time this curve will become stronger, more like Livi's. And her body too will become more curvy in shape than it is now. To him this doesn't matter in the least, not so long as he can be with her to see it happen.

Matt has never been to a festival with a girlfriend before. It's different. Better in some ways. But one odd side-effect is, things are a bit less haphazard than he feels they ought to be. He's used to being last man to crash, and this is no longer the case. Tonight for the second night running he's in his sleeping bag before Shay has even got back to base.

'Wonder what Shay is up to?'

'I thought he was doing his other shift.'

'No, he's on gates tomorrow for the exodus, poor sod. Still, you'd think he'd have sent us a text.'

'Perhaps his battery's flat. He's bound to be back soon,' Ellie says sleepily. Then, 'Say if he's not back by the time we've to pack, what'll we do with his stuff?'

'What stuff?'

He flicks the torch on the other side of the teepee. Not much there. Shay's been taking his guitar around with him in a backpack. The only thing left is that raggedy khaki sleeping bag he's had since they were in scouts.

All evening Shay has been thinking that what he wants most in the world is to be on his own with this girl. Carlita? Carla, maybe. But he can't think of anywhere to go where that is possible. They're both sharing tents with friends, and the festival is not geared up for privacy. In the end she is the one who does something about it. They're walking reluctantly back to the tents when she takes his hand and drags him in a different direction. He's not sure where they're headed until the curve of the double-decker bus looms, and he hears a jangle of keys.

'I'm on earlies tomorrow, so they gave me a key. I reckon the best plan tonight is to stay here.'

There's a pause. She is on the platform, one foot on the stairs. Shay hesitates on the grass outside. She turns.

'You going or staying?'

He leaps aboard and curls his arm around her waist. 'Given the option — I'm staying, of course.'

'Good.'

It's mad busy at the pier the day they leave. Ferries, catamarans, hovercraft — anything that floats has been pressed into service to run an island-to-mainland shuttle from six in the morning till whenever it takes. No one's sure exactly how many thousands of people need to get off the island, but it's a big number. Ellie and Matt pack up at dawn and manage to get themselves on a train home by lunchtime. Shay and the girl still haven't left the campsite by then. She is on brunch duty and he is working a shift on the gates. By the time they finally board a boat to the mainland, it's gone seven.

The boat is small and old fashioned, the elderly crew more used to taking retired couples on harbour tours than shunting music fans across the Solent. Out of habit the skipper steers one-handed and calls out the sights into his microphone. Few of the passengers bother to go on deck and look. Most gather indoors where the comfy seats are, sleeping, or trying to. A guy Shay knows from the sessions at the Chapel mutters, 'What's with the history lesson? We don't need this right now.'

Carla smiles weakly.

Shay is so tired he won't be able to sleep tonight. Maybe he's forgotten how to do sleep. They go outside. The stairs to the top deck wobble underfoot and Shay realises it's not the sea but his own exhaustion making them move. The sea is dotted with forts from forgotten Anglo-Saxon battles that make sense only to the boat's captain. The sight of land is unwelcome: it means the return of the routine, sensible, everyday world.

'I'm going back inside, I'm barely able to stand up.' Carla gestures to his guitar. 'Want me to look after that?'

'It's fine,' Shay says.

It's almost like the guitar is part of him, he can barely feel it anymore, but so she knows he trusts her with it and to keep her with him a moment longer he says, 'Actually, yeah, go on, then,' and shrugs off the backpack.

In this area of the top deck there are no seats, no one near enough to hear them, and he kisses her on the forehead and says shyly, 'I think I love you.' She hugs him hard, as if conscious this may not be possible when they reach the train station on the other side, and mumbles into his chest: 'I know.'

And she's gone.

Shay feels thrown. Does her answer mean she isn't into him? No. It means, do things at your own pace, try not to rush. But it's hard not to feel rushed. They haven't talked much about what will happen back on the mainland, but it won't be easy to stay in touch. Aside from living in different cities, they both live with their parents. And his mum is way less cool than Livi: no way would she let a girl he's just met stay over. But Carla has said, 'If you think it's any different at mine, you've not met my dad.'

Shay is too shattered right now to see a way round this, but there has to be a way. This thing between them, it's important. Put something real like this on hold, let it fizzle out into nothing, and imagine how bad you'd feel. Very. It's like the start of a song that hasn't got going yet. It needs time. They need time.

On the starboard side they must be close to land, for the captain is pointing out the place where they used to load convicts on to prison ships bound for Australia. This side, Shay sees only dusky light on the water. He slips his mobile phone out of his pocket. The last shot he took is a close-up of Carla. He wants a matching shot of himself, now before the glitter and the dirt have rubbed off, as a souvenir of the weekend they first met. There's just enough battery. He clambers on a railing, holds up the phone so the evening sky and the sea will show behind him.

He clicks.

As he's checking to see if the picture came out, the phone slips. He twists his leg, manages to bounce it off his knee so it lands on deck. Phew, one and a half thousand photos saved. And all his numbers.

Then it happens: his feet lose their grip on the rails. He tilts back. In a second he's in a mid-air reverse somersault, like an Olympic show diver but less controlled. He doesn't call out, there's no time for fear, he's just focused on getting out of this. He's thinking it'll be OK right up to the second when the sea beneath him vanishes, replaced by an intense orange mist as his head meets the side of the boat. Dark shapes crowd out the orange, like when he was a small child pushing thumbs on his eyelids to block out the sun. Then the shapes are gone, and after this Shay is not thinking any more.

He does not sense the slick, cold water that opens up, takes hold and softly closes around him. He does not hear the boat chug on without him. He does not even feel the water fill up his air passages, making him more and more heavy until his body gently sinks below the surface.

Carla is asleep when the boat comes to land. She stirs, looks around her at the empty seats, confused, and packs up her things. A crew member watches from nearby, arm raised to indicate the exit route. Where is he? She struggles to lift both her backpack and his guitar. When she reaches the gangplank and finds he's not there she tells the officer, 'My friend, he's up top. He wouldn't leave without me. See — I've got his guitar.'

But the officer blocks her way. 'There's no one up there, love. We always do a headcount, and you're last off.'

Carla is stunned. She can't believe Shay would walk away like this. He really didn't seem the type.

She traipses up the ramp to the train station. No sign of him. And she hasn't got his phone number, so she can't even send him a text. She hurries back, convinced it's a mistake. He's probably curled up asleep somewhere. She'll make them let her on, buy a ticket if she has to. But by the time she reaches the dock, crowds of people are pouring off a huge ferry and the small boat they crossed on is making its way back to the island.

Livi worries about her daughter. This autumn she started her final year of school, but in the weeks since the festival she has been fragile and withdrawn. She stays in her room, rarely going out except for school. When Livi asks what's wrong she swears it's nothing, it's just that no one is going out this year because of the exams.

'Listen, Carlita, I'm worried about you. Don't you trust me enough to tell me what the problem is?'

No reply. Is it something Livi did, or something she failed to do? They were at the festival when all this started. Perhaps she should have told Carlita not to work that last day. Given her a lift home with the band. And than there's that boy she was with the last night. But he had seemed such a nice boy.

'Tell me, is this about your guitar player?'

'What guitar player?'

'The one who asked me the chords to 'Saturday Night'. You remember, at the Undersea Tavern.'

'I met a lot of people at the festival, I don't remember them all now.'

She does remember, Livi's sure of it.

'Isn't that his guitar in your room?'

'That? I bought it off someone at the festival who was short of the train fare home.'

There is a tightness to her daughter's voice that tells Livi it's best to keep out. She has learned the hard way that sometimes this is what she must do.

Carlita hasn't played guitar in a long time. Five or six years. Not since Livi put her up for a school music scholarship. As a child she was a natural, but the day of her audition she asked Livi to stay away. They've never discussed what happened that day. All Livi knows is, she got no scholarship, and later dropped all music lessons.

Now Livi changes the subject to what's for dinner. She knows better than to bring up the topic again, but one day when her daughter is out at school she takes the guitar out of its canvas pack. It sounds just like the one the boy was playing. Looks the same, too.

Still Livi keeps her silence. Even when, as she returns home from an evening out, she hears guitar music coming from upstairs. This happens several times over the next weeks, the music always stopping as soon as she's through the door, and Livi learns to pause before putting her key in the lock. The songs her daughter plays are not ones she has heard before. They are new. Some are happy, some sad, but that is OK. The important thing is, she is playing again.

Airside

I. Take-off – Tasha

Planes always make me feel extra safe and relaxed. Maybe it's that thing with the oxygen masks and the inflatable jackets and those chutes you never get to slide down: it's great the way none of this has changed since I was four years old. OK, so a plane's bigger now and there's more of a fuss over what you can bring on board, but as soon as you strap on your seatbelt you're cocooned in a time-warp world. Nothing else on this planet has stayed the same for ten whole years. I certainly haven't. Not so long ago going to Spain for the summer break was the highlight of my whole year. This year it's been dismal.

We're on our way home and Mum says why don't I watch the in-flight film while she works on her laptop, but I've seen that film before and besides I'm fed up with her telling me what to do, so instead I listen to music. But I'm bored with hearing the same songs over and over so I take off my iPod and make a list on the airplane sick-bag of all the crap things that happened on this holiday.

Spain's OK, I suppose. But I don't speak Spanish so it can get a bit weird for me sometimes. 'My idea of a perfect summer,' I told Mum back when we were planning the holidays, 'is to just laze about at home and hang out with my friends.'

'We tried that at Easter. You barely saw them.'

Annoyingly, Mum is right. Whenever I contacted my school friends about meeting up, the messages that came back told me they were off surfing in Cornwall, or at some stupid camp, or in Scotland visiting their gran. One of them even went to the Caribbean. So that was that. Mum bought tickets for Spain as usual and out we came.

Two other English kids, Jamie and Sara, have a summer place in the village. Other summers I hung out with them, but this trip their house was barred and shuttered, the garden dry and dusty. Maybe they sold up, or their folks got divorced, or something. But those kids were, like, never the top thing about Spain. What used to be cool about it was when I was little and me and Mum would be all by ourselves with no work and no school, without even a telly. We did stuff we'd never do at home. Invent games, paint pictures, go out walking, learn to cook tortilla. Once, we made little animals out of driftwood and shells we found on the shore.

Only, this trip, Mum was too busy for all that. A few days in, she had broadband installed and after that she was online for hours every day. It just wasn't like a holiday anymore. She only went to the beach every two or three days — too long a drive, she said. That's so lame. I mean, why come all this way just so you can work?

'Swim at the outdoor pool here in the village,' Mum said, 'then you are free to come and go as you please.'

For years we drove past that pool to the sea, never once stopping. The bad news is that under-sixteens get in free, and since Mum found this out she has kept on about how I should make the most of it. But I hate being there by myself while the Spanish kids hang out together laughing at jokes I don't get, so I spent most of my holiday up in my room listening to music.

It's been a very long three weeks.

After I finish writing the list I start to rip shreds of paper off the sick bag. Then I take out my phone and just sit there fiddling with it, guessing how many new texts I'll have when I'm finally allowed switch it back on, and hoping some of my friends will actually be around tomorrow. Mum snaps at me to 'Put that damn thing away' or some lame parenty thing like that. Whatever.

I hate her. I wish we'd never even gone on this holiday. I don't know how yet, but somehow I'm going to get out of going to Spain next year.

II. Flight – Jeannot

Is good to be fast. Speed is what they pay us for here in Gatwick. If a plane come late we clean super-fast, until it taxi away so shiny it hurt your eye. Now is early-early, maybe six thirty, near the start of my shift. Soon will come many plane, clack-clack-clack, one after the next.

Me and Gil, we work the same shift. Twelve hours, from six in the morning to six at night. One of us clean from front of plane, one from back, till we meet somewhere between. Before, in Mauritius, we work together with fibreglass, making speedboat. Some days me and Gil would get up at dawn and go fishing before work. Everybody in Mauritius go fishing, is not something special like here. Best time is early-early when the sea is quiet. Mauritius don't have too many fish, not like the old island, and if you fish for your job like Uncle Eric, you must go out pass the reef, and stay out long time — maybe five day, maybe two week. Until you get fish.

Is hard work, Old Eric say. On Diego Garcia, he would catch fish so easy he never leave the lagoon. But even Diego don't have so much fish no more, Eric say. We can't go there now, is forbidden, but Old Eric talk like he know. Maybe he been there in secret some night while the soldier sleeping. The reef all break up, he say, and the village is jungle. And where is copra plantation before, now is a concrete runway.

I reach under the window seat, pick up many small piece of white paper that the hoover refuse to eat. Outside, people get off the next plane all suntan and summer shirt, coming home. Every day they leave behind many-many small thing: book, make-up, camera. Last week I find passport. British passport, under a First Class blanket. A man, maybe fifty years old. So I radio supervisor because maybe they put this man in that prison for people with no identity. I know about this place because sometimes when families come from Mauritius to visit, they are not allowed to pass inside England. The custom officer turn them around and send them home again on the next plane, and in between they can go nowhere, they must wait in that room. But supervisor tell me the man pass with other ID, she send on his passport by post. He must be very important, this man. Or very rich, maybe.

All week I hope for reward, but nothing come.

I drop all the piece of white paper in my rubbish bag, then start on the seat pocket. I fish out something small and hard. An iPod. So small is hard to believe it hold many-many song. Must be broke, I think. But I press a button and the sound is perfect. Is not right what I do, but I see again the photo of that man in the passport: a man who expect much from life, who look so sure that everything he take is for him. Maybe I need to be more sure, too. I slip the player in my pocket and pass through Economy row by row until I find Gil at the wing.

Me and Gil did not want this kind of work. Cleaning is a work for women. Still, we earn more money now than before, when we made speedboat.

I want to tell Gil about the music player, but at the end I say nothing. Better he don't know about it, just in case the supervisor catch me.

People say that here in Crawley we're still close to the sea, is just one hour away. But England is big island: they mean one hour by car, not by foot. Since we come to live here I never see the sea. But I know it is here. When is storm, seagull fly overhead and the wind smell of salt. Then this whole town feel like an island we stuck on, like the real England is far far away. Is maybe a place on television, a land we never reach.

III. Touchdown – Maycel

My new school is ginormous. It has a gym, and science labs, language labs and everything. It even has small rooms away from class where I take special English lessons, the first month or two. My first day I couldn't say nothing, couldn't understand nothing, because in Mauritius all our lessons was in French. I just sat in a corner and at the end of each lesson the teacher told me in French where to go to next, so I didn't get lost.

When I'm on to sentences, my English teacher gives me a homework essay: do I like England, or not, she asks. I love it. In Mauritius we lived in two rooms, all six of us. Here we have a house with an upstairs and a downstairs, like we're rich. My brothers share a room but I have a bedroom to myself, because my sister get marry two months ago and go to live in her marriage house. My dad says England is his third island and it will be his last. He is from Diego Garcia. For me England is my second island. I hope to see Diego one day, but there's so many places I want to see. I want to see the whole world.

After I been at my new school a while I made new friends and went round their houses for birthday parties, so I see that, like, next to them we're not rich, even if it feels like we are. Anyway we're not, you know, Posh and Becks rich, but we're not poor neither, never like before.

One thing I miss here is the sea. In Mauritius we went out on my dad's boat most weekends, and cooked fresh fish over a fire on the beach. Dad still finds it hard to sleep without hearing the waves. I told him the cars at night sound a bit like waves, and he just looked at me, sad. He wants to bring us to the seaside. He's bought maps to plan where to go, but we don't have no car so he says we must wait for the summer holidays.

My birthday is in summer term, on the day of our school trip. We bring a pack-lunch, and go on a big old double-decker bus, singing songs the whole way. When I get home after, there's a cake with thirteen candles and a tiny present. I think of the girls at school, their huge parties and stacks of presents, and wonder what's inside. I open it and see. An iPod. I don't believe it.

I hug my dad, put in the phones. He's put Sega music on the memory, and the shop must have helped choose because there's other stuff here, too. New songs that I know he has never heard.

'So how was your school trip?' my dad asks. 'Where did you go?'

'The seaside. It was great.'

He looks at me strangely then, and pulls out his maps and asks, 'Which sea you go to? Brighton, with the stones?' He points at a photo of a beach with big round stones instead of sand, like the stones English people put in their gardens to hide the weeds.

'Another beach. With small stones but sand as well.'

He runs his finger along the map and reads out names but none of them sounds right: Hastings, Bexhill, Bognor Regis, Selsey, Wittering. 'Tell me, is it a big old castle there, or not?' But I don't know, so I say nothing.

When I was little my dad told me about his island: how Diego has a reef all round to keep it safe, and water foams softly on the reef day and night, like the breathing of a magical world. In and out, in and out.

Now he looks sad as he puts away his maps.

'It wasn't like our ocean, Dad,' I tell him. 'The water was so cold that nobody went swimming.'

Because of my birthday, Dad lets me go to the big party on Saturday night. The weather has changed. It's hot tonight, and everybody from the islands is here. Mums and grandmas sit gossiping, eating chicken drumsticks and sweetcorn. When the music change to Sega and their daughters come on stage, they stand up, smiling, to take photos. The hall is jammed with dancers and suddenly it's so hot that I push through the crowd to the door, looking for cool air. It's mostly men outside, talking and smoking. My dad is with friends, so I just wave. The man with him looks like his uncle, but it can't be. Old Eric has gone back to Mauritius to celebrate there.

He came for the court case about Diego. He stayed in our house and every day he travelled in a bus to the High Court in London with the other old people. How was it today, we'd ask him each evening.

'Just another day of the long long talk of the men of law. One man talk for the Queen, one for the island,' Old Eric said. 'We see only their backs, each in a black cloak and white wig. It's hard to tell which is which, because from their voices and clothes, they could be twins.'

My brother asked what the men of law could find to say all this time.

'The men in wigs use long, long words that suck their meaning dry. One thing I see: each day they stop talking at exactly quarter to one. Then the frown-face judge bang his hammer and say "All rise", and we must stand while the three of them leave by a private door to take their lunch.' Old Eric shrugged, and out of his sun-dried raisiny face came a high-pitched giggle like the girls at school. Soon he had us giggling too at those silly men in wigs.

I know this is just a patch of unused land out past the community centre, but it's the end of our little world: a place where the houses and shops just fade away. I walk with my iPod on random letting it mix up old songs with new. Dad beckons but I pretend not to see. I'm right on the edge of the party here and I want to enjoy this feeling. Long grass rolls back like dunes, and the cars parked on it have their doors open, all different musics pouring out, many small parties clustered around the big party in the hall.

Before he left, Old Eric told us this: the judge says we can go back to Chagos if we want. My father never speaks of going back. He is tired of moving, he wants to stay here. Or maybe he doesn't believe the men of law because they have said this before, and they keep changing their story. This is what I think of as I pace beneath the red glow where the sun was a minute ago, as I walk between the cars, feeling the grass give under my feet.

In a gap between songs something makes me look up. A small plane, too far away to hear, pulls a cloud across a pink sky. I hear the soft white noise of saltwater foaming on coral. In and out. In and out. Breaths. Like that moment when the seawater draws back from shore, holding its breath, and finally crashes on the sand, foaming around your feet in tiny bubbles that tickle as they burst and pull away. We may be one hour from the coast, from Brighton or those other seas, but tonight we magic the waves to us. Tonight we make a beach party.

God Mode

Changing planes at Schiphol it comes back to me, this feeling of having been drag-and-dropped into a looped game sequence. I step on a moving walkway and watch the airport scroll by. The silver pathway glides towards a cluster of bars and See Buy Fly shops that could be copy-and-pastes of those at the end of the previous walkway, or the one before that. I'm trapped within the pixelated confines of an oversized game world, but to get where I want to be this is a level I must pass through. Mindful of the win condition, I weave a course between the shadowy passengers on the walkway, all the time keeping my eyes on those bright yellow arrows pointing to the departure gate.

Level I – archaic

Last time I passed through, the time I met the woman from Santorini, I was en route for Skiathos. This ten-day holiday would have been our first time going away together for more than a weekend, but the previous night Max announced flatly that he wouldn't be coming. He was seeing someone else.

My flatmate Jan said to cancel but I'd booked my leave and paid my ticket, so off I went, unsure if I was doing the right thing. As I wandered around the shopping area I noticed a book:

Get Over Him in 10 Days. Flicking through the book, I liked its calm instructive tone, the soothing certainty it offered. It was on a 3-for-2. Finding nothing to go with it, I stocked up instead on books I'd always wanted to read but had never got around to. History, an atlas of the night sky, a dozen novels, even a new children's series that I liked the look of. Soon my overfull basket was on the counter and I was listening to the blip of the barcode scanner while I waited to pay. Each blip added another weapon against Max — this small library might give me a cheat code for the game we'd been playing. If I got through this trip without thinking about him, I'd be home safe, able to restart my life with no major damage.

I met Anna on board the plane.

At supper she spoke to me across the gap left by his empty seat. For a while I kept my thumb between the pages of my book, waiting for an out-point. It never came. She kept talking, moving swiftly from a comment on airplane food to the medical condition that limited her diet.

'. . . a routine operation, but afterwards I felt worse than before. Phantom pain my doctor called it, didn't believe me until he saw the X-ray.' Her hand made an apple shape in the air. 'That big it was, made of metal — a clamp left in my belly. Surgeon forgot to clear up after himself, like a painter who leaves used paint-cans about the house.'

I felt mean then for having wished she would stop talking, and searched for some positive and reassuring response. There was none. Her intestine was so badly damaged part of it needed cutting away. They were patching her up, but she'd never be the same.

Then just as suddenly Anna changed tack and spoke of life on her island, how she loved Thira in the winter when it was empty and the seas were wild. I'd never been there, although it's the sort of place that people say you must *do*, like Delphi or the Acropolis. I'd seen pictures: the vines rooted in ashes; the vast ragged circle of the bay; the white buildings strewn like spilt sugar on a cliff that is the edge of a dead volcano. But I preferred quieter, less famous islands. Still, her enthusiasm was infectious, and I set aside my book to listen. And when we reached Athens I helped her to carry the many packages she had stowed in the overhead locker — wine and cheese fresh from France, to share with her girlfriends.

'We'll kick my husband out the house and have a rare old time,' she said, smiling. For a moment I wished I could be there. Although I hadn't wanted to listen, I knew that I'd miss the sound of her voice as soon as she was gone.

She gave me a hug.

'If you ever visit Thira, come and stay. Just ask for Anna from the paint shop, everyone knows me.'

And we flew away, each to her own island.

People on Skyros were friendly, but I was in no mood to be friendly back. My few words of Greek (*ya sass, to kotopoulo parakalo, kalinichta*) were enough for the locals; when tourists addressed me I shook my head and said 'Me, Slovakia.' Unconvincing, perhaps, given my arsenal of books was in English, but I needed time to myself.

Problem was, an after-image of Max hovered in the same frame as me, waiting to attack when he found a moment. I'd close my eyes against the sun and hear him pick out the cutest woman on the beach, then ask why she was wasting her time with the dodgy bloke next to her. If I looked where the voice was coming from, he'd be sprawled on the sand next to me.

Max often used to point out women to me, before. 'Hey, she's cute,' he'd say. And I didn't mind. I thought he was teasing me. But in truth it was all about fixing the limits of his game. Letting me know that there would always be the girl after me, and the girl after her, and so on. Each a little sushi dish to nibble on so as to conserve appetite for the next.

When Max launched his attacks I would dive into the salty blue sea and swim down to a place where his jibes were wiped from the soundtrack and all I could see were rocks and fish. Later, I'd walk back along the dusty path to the village and eat dinner under the guise of an afternoon snack. Nights I'd stay in and read until the words were shoals of letters that swam off the page; often I'd wake with the edge of a book imprinted on my face. This at least made it hard for Max to get in. I remember vividly the one time he did manage it. That night halfway through the holiday when I closed my eyes and saw him, one arm around some girl in skinny jeans and half a T-shirt, strolling through Amsterdam or Bolivia or Bethnal Green, a proud grin on his face that showed he knew standing next to her made him look ten years younger.

I jumped up and went out on the balcony. It was late at night and many of the town lights were dimmed. Overhead for once the Milky Way really did blaze a white trail across the navy sky. I fetched my night sky atlas. Matching the stars overhead to the constellation diagrams, I picked out Sirius and Cassiopeia, the Plough, and a little cluster called the Pleiades or the Seven Sisters. All night I memorised stars until Max was galaxies away.

I didn't see him again the whole rest of the holiday.

On the last day, when my literary stash had served its purpose, I added it to the paperbacks left behind by previous hotel guests. It took some doing, but I made space for every book. Some had to rough it next to Nordic crime novels and a yellowed *Rough*

Guide to the Islands, others found loftier dwellings on the top shelf, in between a copy of *The Name of the Rose* with sand in its swollen pages, and a first edition biography of Kierkegaard.

Level II – classical

At home I gave Jan a bottle of duty free ouzo, and we invited Emily and Catriona over for cocktails. We mixed ouzo with everything — cranberry, coke, lemonade, even coffee — but nothing blocked out the liquorice taste. Late in the evening when the line between fantasy and reality started to blur, someone asked, 'What's the worst thing you've done to get even with some-body else?'

Catriona had poured Nitromors on Paul's Karmen Ghia coupé. She laughed. 'He spent a month of Sundays scraping, sanding and repainting.'

'That gorgeous car — Cat, how could you?'

'Slashed the back seat, an' all.'

'No, you didn't?'

'Needed fresh leather on that seat,' Catriona said, 'before he used it to get it on with his new bint.'

Laughing, we turned to Jan, expecting to hear at least one good story. She said, 'Nothing to tell. Call it attention deficit dis-order, I get through men so fast they never have a chance to piss me off.'

Emily had been quiet. Now she cracked. 'Remember Charles?' she asked.

How could we not? Ems and Charles, Charles and Ems, their names twined together for over a decade ever since school. Everyone had expected them to get married. Then a year ago it was all over. Emily had barely mentioned him since.

'Go on, Ems, what did you do?'

'Kept his apartment keys.'

'And?'

'You know he got married last month? I went over while he was on honeymoon. There was an under offer sign out front. They're moving to the suburbs, I saw it on his Facebook. I was going to trash the place, but then I had a better idea: I stole the title deeds.'

Shouts of laughter gave way to puzzled silence. Catriona asked, 'You can't actually sell the place though, can you?'

'Nope. Just want to make him squirm.'

More laughter. I took some plates and glasses into the kitchen. When I got back everyone was staring at me.

'What?'

They carried on staring.

'If you mean Max, I've been on holiday since we broke up. What could I possibly have done?'

'Charged it to the joint account,' Jan offered.

'I was with him six months, you think we even had a joint account?'

'Cyber crime, then?'

'I didn't want to waste time thinking about him.'

This was the edited version. If I'd told them a hologram Max had trailed me around Greece, talking to me every time I took my head out of a book, they'd have said I was nuts. Must have been the sun, right?

Later, when Ems and Catriona had gone home and Jan was asleep, I sat up with the lights out and curtains open, watching for stars. Thought I'd try to remember their names, but the sky had that orangey purple glow it takes on when half the city's sleeping and the other half is partying through the night. London's like that sometimes. When I was little and my cousin from Ireland came to stay, she woke up one night terrified of the huge fire in the sky. Took Mum ages to calm her down. On nights when the clouds glow orange like that, you can't see a single star. I dozed awhile. When I woke, the clouds had thinned out and a few tiny lights were winking at me. The Pleiades, all huddled together in a tight little gang.

From time to time over the following months the girls gave me updates, or I pieced together bits of what Max was up to from photos that had been posted online. 'Max broke up with what's-her-name, the Australian,' Emily told me. 'They had a massive row halfway across Asia. After Phnom Penh they went their separate ways.' The news did not come as a surprise, but my reaction to it did. I didn't gloat, just felt mildly sorry for the Australian woman. That was about it, really.

A while later they started talking about the new girlfriend he brought back. I suppose no one had mentioned her before in case it upset me. Apparently she used to be a tour guide at Angkor Wat. That's how they met. He posted a whole album of her talking into a microphone on the tour bus. Lovely face. They got engaged so as to wangle her a six-month entry visa, but a month after landing in England she vanished. Smart woman. Got her visa and got out.

Word was, Max was gutted. It was two months later, coming up to Christmas, when I finally got the call. Jan glowered as she handed me the phone.

'Maxxx,' she hissed.

I took the phone and waited.

'Hello, you.'

Said like it was six hours since we'd spoken, not six months.

'How you doing?' I replied, aiming for a cool tone although my heart hammered out a rhythm that was anything but.

'I'm good. But I miss you, little one, d'you know that?'

I couldn't help being pleased. Pleased again when he said how nice it would be to spend some time together over the Christmas.

All that distance I thought I'd travelled, all that discipline, and here I was gearing up to let him start over in exactly the same place. A tiny point of light winked for my attention, don't do this, don't let him use you to plug a gap in his diary, but I didn't want to know. After all Max has been through, I thought, after all the time he's taken to reflect on things, he must feel more sure about me. About us. Before I hung up it was all arranged.

Level III – heroic

So here I am again, three days before Christmas, navigating the airport, following the little yellow arrows for Gate 74, hoping this time I'll move up a level. In real life there are no cheat codes, no god modes, no back-up lives. You just have the one life, and you have to make the most of it, like I'm trying to do now.

I'm not sure Max really gets this, I'm thinking, as the duty free shops scroll by. But maybe that's not his fault; maybe he is the way he is on account of his mum running off when he was little. Usually it's the dads who run off, isn't it? With him it was his mum. He thinks the world of her, but she's very distant, only rarely letting him into her orbit. I'm near the end of the walkway, the yellow arrows for my gate pretty close, when my phone goes. The call is not unexpected, but all the same it makes me start and I jostle the passenger in front, earning a mean glare.

I press the green button and say hello.

'Champagne's in the fridge, little one. What's up? Thought you'd be here by now.'

'I'm not coming, Max.'

'Come on, it's too close to Christmas, you can't change plans now.'

His voice is mild, reasonable. Listen, and I might relent.

'You are coming, aren't you? It's all arranged.'

'Sorry Max, I just can't.'

This is the game Max is trapped in: playing freefall with an endless series of women. Each time one of them trusts him enough to relax, he lets go and she crashes to earth; then he takes it from the top with someone new. The win condition is simple. Be first to let go. Not a game I want to play any more, but this is the only way I know of properly ending it.

'What about us?' he says. 'It's Christmas.'

'I have to go.'

It's last call for my flight. I wish him a happy new year as I hand in my boarding pass.

The connecting flight out of Schiphol takes two hours, maybe two and a half, then there's a short local flight that leaves Athens at dawn. A small plane that flies close to the sea, skimming the islands. Sunlight prises its way into the cabin, a welcome guest arrived too soon. In a superhuman effort to stay awake I borrow a guidebook from a fellow passenger. The little plane's engines are improbably loud for its size, and after a while, dizzy from rapid doses of history and geology, I let the book fall.

I dream of the island I'm flying to. Anna's island. Covered in ash thousands of years old, its coastline rises from the depths too steeply to have allowed beaches to form, and I'm in a rocky cove unlike any I've seen before. The sand, if you can call it sand, is dark grey and dotted with lumps of black rock or coal. Tourists sprawl on charred wooden lilos, roasting their flesh in the burning sun. I don't like it here. Then the beach is not a beach any more but a vineyard, high up in a place where the land makes one long slope towards the sea. I stand in a queue of people waiting for a wine tasting. The man ahead of me extols the wine's rejuvenating properties, then takes off his sunglasses to show how well it's worked for him.

I panic. It's Max.

Older, and with bloodshot evil eyes. But Max.

He cannot be here, he doesn't even know where I am.

I dart off the path into the field, stumble past rows of stunted vines that are not trained on supports but rest on the powdery dirt, their brown grapes wrinkled like raisins. It's hard to believe any wine worth drinking could come of this shrivelled fruit. With each step, my foot sinks into ashy earth, like walking on fresh snow. Or moon dust, maybe.

I glance back.

A towering Max is following me.

Clingy dust sucks at my feet so I can barely move.

He laughs at my futile efforts to escape. I glance back and he doubles in size. Looking at him is clearly a mistake. It gives him power. I turn and hunt desperately for a way out, but the rows of vines repeat forever. It's a maze.

In the distance I see Anna, and call her name.

She doesn't hear me so I run after her, or try to. She walks towards her car with ease while I manage only a slow inelegant shuffle. As I get closer to her it becomes easier to move, and I reach the road in time to see her car disappear around a bend.

Now that I'm safely off the ashen ground, I dare to glance back one last time. A distant zombie Max wriggles on the spot behind a row of vines. Still ghoulish but no longer a threat, just a 2-D avatar lost in an ill-defined game area.

Level IV – mythic

When I wake, the plane has landed and I'm sweating. There are two new messages on my phone, both from Max. I delete them unread. He can't follow me here, I won't let him.

We never swapped addresses, but finding Anna is easy. I take a taxi from the airport to the paint shop.

'*Yassou paidi mou*,' she says. 'You choose very nice time to visit. Winter, my favourite time.'

I tell her I'll stay at a hotel but she takes my bag and puts it in her car. She asks 'Did you watch the landing?'

'I was asleep.'

'Good, then you're coming out on a boat with me today. It's the best way to see Thira.'

In Anna's car, before we begin the steep descent to the port, she pulls over. 'We should cover your eyes,' she says, pulling a hairband over my head.

I look at her, puzzled.

'So you see the bay at the best moment,' she slips the band over my eyes.

'I'll just look the other way,' I say, worried that Max could reappear.

But Anna clucks dismissively and puts the car in gear.

With the blindfold on, the journey to the port is like radio. We swing downhill on a series of exaggerated hairpin bends until finally the road levels out. The car stops and the driver window hums open. I hear water slapping a sea wall, a burst of conversation. Anna's voice a bright interrogative patter, and in response a man's lazy negative drawl: '*Oxi. Thehlo perisottero kosmo.*'

He wants more people.

Or maybe, he wants more world?

The Greek words for people and world sound the same to me, and I think, Yes, I want more world too. I learnt these words on another trip when I stayed in Neoskosmos, Athens. 'New World' seemed a good omen until I opened my balcony door and petrol fumes wafted in from the car repair shop down at street level. Not the New World I was looking for.

Anna says something more and I catch only her tone, like a mother telling off a small child. The boatman clicks his teeth and growls, '*Then ftahni.*'

Water slaps at the wall.

'He waits more people,' she explains. 'Santorini is empty, so I ask him to take just us and those three Japanese girls. But he says it's not worth it.'

A few minutes pass, ten, fifteen. Then another car comes. Rapid speech between two men, the slam of car doors, thunk-thonk of feet on wood.

'*Endaxi, pahme,*' the boatman says.

Anna opens my door. 'Time to go.'

'I'll look silly with a blindfold on,' I protest.

She opens the dash, then rests something heavy on my face. 'My wraparound driving shades. They cover it completely.'

She takes my hand, helps me from the car and guides me aboard. The engine starts. When we're seated she whispers, 'Patience. Not long now.'

I listen to the thrum of the engine, the churn of salt water.

After some time she stands me up and removes the glasses and blindfold.

Light floods in.

Anna lets me watch in silence. It is the sheer scale of this place I'm unprepared for. We are out in the centre of a bay so wide it feels like open sea. Distant cliffs rise hundreds of feet into the sky in a ragged semicircle around us. Above the port, the town appears flattened, its squat white buildings like sugarcubes spilt on dark rocks. I can't imagine a volcanic eruption this huge.

'When was it last active?' I ask eventually.

'Half of Fira fell down in a quake in 1956. Many people left after that. My parents too: they got married and left for Australia.'

Anna told me on the plane about growing up in Oz, too short and dark to be a 'real Australian'. About coming here for the first time, how she fell in love with the sky, the stars, the rocks. And with her husband, in that order.

She looks at me. 'The really huge explosions were hundreds of thousands of years ago. They think the last big one was quite recent: three and a half thousand years. Scientists say it could have been ten times the size of Krakatoa.'

Behind her the cliff face is layers of chocolate, coffee, and walnut, topped with vanilla. A giant's birthday cake.

'Did many people live here then?' I ask.

'You've heard of the lost city of Atlantis?'

'Of course.'

'Well, right here in this bay is where it was. An island within the crater. Once, the scientists said it was far from here, but they changed their minds. It fits because Thira's ancient name was "round".'

'So the people of Atlantis were living right in the mouth of a volcano?'

'Exactly.'

'Then crash, bang, tsunami, chaos . . .' I shudder.

Anna does not react.

'So,' I ask, 'why did the scientists change their minds?'

'New evidence, they said. Such a *fasaria* they made. One lot sent undersea robots to measure lava. Another dug up the buried town at Akrotiri. They held press conferences, and each claimed their research "proved" Atlantis was here.'

'And you? Did you believe them?'

Anna gazes into the sea. 'Me, I felt sure Atlantis was here, even before they said it.'

'Why?'

'Atlantis was close to heaven. As Thira is too.'

The boat stops at a small rocky island. The boatman coughs and switches on a small microphone. 'Here you see a new island, only one or two centuries old, still growing,' he says, and I wonder if future people who have lost the old stories will make the error of living here. 'Sorry, today is no time for full tour, we must hurry for the tide. You have fifteen minutes to look around.'

Anna raises her eyes to heaven; it's not the tide but reduced ticket sales which led to the change of plan, her look suggests. The Japanese girls press ahead towards the crater, light footed in their skate shoes despite the ankle twisting terrain. We stumble after them. Behind us the Americans coagulate close to the boat, examining lumps of volcanic rock.

As we walk I ask Anna, 'Haven't they been digging up Akrotiri for years? Why change their theories now?'

'I don't know,' she says, her voice strained. 'Maybe after the tsunami they were better able to picture things. The wave that crashed down, taking with it all it could.'

And there would have been plenty to take. The Minoans built

on sea level, no walls around their towns. Theirs was a peaceful civilisation, it had no need of walls.

'Maybe fear of a tsunami is why they built the villages so high on the hillsides of Greek islands?'

'Could be. Pirates were one threat, the sea was another. Is another . . . A lesson we forget, these days.'

This talk of ancient disasters makes me think of a computer game me and the girls used to play: Age of Mythology. AoM we called it for short. At the start you each get one village. To move up through the levels you build temples, villages, a market, an armoury. If your army is big enough you don't need to farm, you can steal crops from others. An addictive game. We played at Catriona's flat each night for a fortnight until she begged us to take the game and play it elsewhere. I still remember the sound effects: digital waves breaking on a two-dimensional shore, the workers shouting *mallista*, the crash as one player's god-power unleashes disaster on an enemy: a thunderbolt, an earthquake, or a tidal wave.

Anna sits on a rock heavily, suddenly tired.

'You go on to the crater, I will wait here,' she says.

'It's fine.'

We are closer to the crater, there's a hint of sulphur in the air. If she rests awhile, maybe we can still get there.

But it is time: the boatman calls us back.

We wave at the Japanese girls in the distance and point to the boat, then pick our way across lumps of rusted lava lying in the heaps they were spewed up in, decades ago. The elderly Americans wait on board, their backpacks weighed down with rock samples. Reluctantly the Japanese girls come skittering back from the crater's edge, their playful fragile bodies looking like they've sprung from the pages of a comic book.

The boat chugs across turquoise shallows. I ask Anna, 'How does it feel to live on the edge of all this? Do you not worry it could happen again?'

Her silence tells me I should not have asked.

The boat picks up speed. It's windy going across the bay, the water dark navy broken by foaming white-caps. A wave breaks against the side of the boat and sends spray across the deck. Drops of saltwater chill my face.

'I don't know if I could live with that uncertainty.'

Anna looks at me a long second. Is she thinking that everywhere has its bad points, dangers that people living there can't or won't see? Is she bored? She probably makes this trip with every visitor. Do they all say the same things as me?

'You know, a fault line runs right through Greece. Everybody can't leave. And anyway, all of life is like that.'

'Like what?'

'I mean, at any point something bad can happen. Like what happened to me: the surgeon who made a mistake.'

I feel guilty. I'd almost forgotten.

She raises the camera and takes a picture of Oia, an old town on the far side of the crater that escaped the last quake. 'When something really bad happens, it can't be fixed. But you learn to live another kind of life, around the edges, you know?'

I glance at the pixels stored on her camera, then look up at the real thing: the houses facing into the caldera all golden now with the kiss of the evening sun, so calm and perfect they look as if nothing bad can ever touch them.

Outer Banks Riptide

DUNE | The beach smells so hot and dry and salty you'd think summer will never fade, and yet it's August so it can't stay like this forever. Can it? Jude lies next to Gabriel, their bodies not quite touching, the smooth skin of his back filling her horizon. After they finished surfing the two of them flopped on the dune to catch some lazy afternoon sun, but the Atlantic keeps on rolling. Day or night, it never tires. And Jude never tires of hearing it. Her energy's dropped now for quite another reason: Gabriel has said he's leaving the Outer Banks.

She should have known. After all, he's only a summer islander. His family has an oceanfront beach house so he's here every summer, but this year he was on probation at college and he told her if he didn't make his retakes, he'd stay on awhile. Find a job. Learn how to build boats or fix houses — something well paid he could do in the off season. Only now he's got through. And being realistic, how would he have stayed? Come winter, the oceanfront side of the island is windy as all hell, empty beach houses rattling and pinging like a marina in a storm. A few hardy souls return at Thanksgiving, much as anything to tie down their homes and keep them from blowing away. Jude and her mom live over soundside, the width of the island between them and the ocean. Away from the fray.

Jude is conscious of Gabriel waiting for her reply. Thinks she'll get riled, maybe. Or forgive him. But she won't do either of those things: it's up to him what he chooses. She grabs a fistful of sand and lets it trickle on his back, tracing letters on his pale skin. I-L-O, then with another scoop of sand V-E-D, and Y-O-. She wonders can he tell them by the feel of the sand. Gabriel twitches, then sits up, and the words tumble away. All that's left is a pinch of sand that careens off him as he wrestles her to make her stop. But he's laughing. They both are.

—What?

—I'll miss you, boy.

—And I'll miss you.

Their eyes inches apart, searching.

Against her will Jude turns serious.

—No way I'm gonna leave here. But I could visit.

—Not that I want to put you off or anything, but . . .

He grins and a crinkle line appears where the sun has dried the skin around his eyes, a line that his soft winter life will soon rinse away. She finishes for him,

—But you want to put me off.

He looks embarrassed then, which is something, at least.

—Not exactly. But, well, Cornell's another world. You belong here. And much as I like you, I need to fit in there.

—And a visit from me will stop you?

—I'm sorry. Come visit if you want, I was just saying . . .

—Forget it. I'll have work most weekends, anyway.

The tension fades from his face.

—How about I visit you. Chances are I'll be down at Thanksgiving.

Yeah, at the beach house with your entire family, she thinks.

Two actual genetic parents, a brother, a sister, even a dog. That *is* another world.

—Might be best not to make plans, Gabe. Just let it go.

—Summer's not done yet.

Again that line as he smiles. Their kisses banish the future, bury it under a heap of here and now, under the yellowy August sun. The wind whips their faces and stings their skin as they lean into the sand, and into each other.

JOCKEY'S RIDGE | Up above Jockey's Ridge a few herons are flying south. One bird is finding it tough to keep up. It struggles awhile, then finally drops down onto the massive sandy ridge that traverses the island, and that migrates south each year, inch by inch, when the northerlies blow. Kill Devil Hill once used to move south too, but the men who erected the Wright memorial grassed it over and locked it down, burying the very thing that had drawn the Wright brothers there in the first place: the soft landing surface of the dune. From its spot on the ridge the straggler calls out to the other birds, telling them it's stuck in a strange yellow world with no trees and no grass and no water. But they have worries of their own, and do not heed its calls. The young bird watches them grow smaller and smaller and finally fade into the sky. All the while it keeps its beak pointed after them, hoping to follow.

BEACH HOUSE | It is early when the seabirds start their morning chores. They tend to burble on more when it's clear, so Hugo heeds their advice and gets up. An impressive dawn. Gold ribbons slung across the sky. He stands on the deck a long time, wide-eyed and still, as if to scorch the colours on his retinas. He is training himself out of the urge to photograph such things. Doing so reduces them to failed pixels, to some sort of diagram of a sunrise, *Oh yes I remember that day, it was gorgeous.* Yes. Gorgeous and volatile and real. In a way that a tiny photo saved to his phone or posted on some website never can be. Anyway his phone is dead by now, for all he knows. Hugo is meant to check his messages in case anything crops up at work, but it's surprising how swiftly the habit of it recedes. Voicemail, tweets, texts. None of that stuff matters out here. Life on the Outer Banks is bigger, more elemental. Just him and the sky, the ocean.

BEACH | Construction vehicles grumble and grind at an urgent job crammed between summer and the high winds, leaving their tracks behind them like giant zippers in the sand. An offshore wind has blown the sands clear of tourists and whipped up a sudden flock of surfers. All summer whenever a swell got up, photographers in charter boats hovered on the flat water just inside break point; now they're gone, the surfers finally have a clear run. Jude's not been out on the water these past weeks since Gabriel left, but still she gauges the surf. Not a bad swell for round here: three, maybe four foot. Gabriel would love it.

The thought of him curls around in her head like scum on water, and she makes herself stop. It's the only way.

She keeps walking. The workers are cranking up an old cedar-wood beach house, perhaps to mount it on taller stilts, or haul it back from shore. Nothing out of the way really, just another sign of Fall. The Outer Banks change shape year on year, and almost since they first built here people have had to be ready to move it or lose it, when the ocean gets too close. A lesson learned when the Underground Railroad hut and the old Lifeboat Station were lost to the sea. Jude walks on past the house to an empty stretch of sand where the generator noise is snatched away by the wind.

She doesn't mind seeing the island empty out. It could use some quiet time. Kill Devil Hills feels more like itself when it's quiet. Her boss at the Outer Banks Brewing Station has asked is she good to work three shifts a week through the winter, Friday through Sunday. Of course she is. It's one of the few bars that's open year-round, and three shifts a week is better than none. Weekdays she splits between drawing comics and a morning job that keeps her in funds.

Out on the point, Jackson, a guy she knows from her shifts at the Brewing Station, speeds along a wave. Jude knows it's him because of his bright orange stick, an Aloha. He crouches into the tube and disappears from view, pushing out into the foam at the far end, still upright. She grins. They're all in body-suits but him. Jackson's not one to let a bitty gust of wind blow him out of the water.

RESTAURANT, MANHATTAN | They're having team lunch at that old school restaurant at the Rockefeller, the place Paul always chooses when he's buying. It's late. They've stayed on too long, raising an extra toast to celebrate the fact the shoot's done and the show in edits, when finally Paul tweezers it out of him. It only takes a second, and straightaway Hugo knows it's a mistake to have said it. Only since taking on the beach house people keep asking if he's in love, and he says no it's not that, and Paul says what is it then because I want some, and he goes and opens his big mouth . . .

—You spent how much again?

—Doesn't matter, Paul, it's worth every cent.

—On some sort of tree-house? No wait, a giant balsa wood sandcastle. My god, Hugo, that's immense.

Hugo glances around hoping no one else is listening.

—Doesn't it bother you that the next big storm that blows up to North Carolina could make hurricane snacks of your beach-front house?

—Uh, not really, no.

Paul really ought to get this. In about ten minutes, he's going to pay two or three times what this lunch is worth just because he ate it in his favourite restaurant. But the weird thing is, when Paul asks why he so likes his beach house on stilts, he's no good at putting it in words. He can't define its magic any more than his in-phone camera can capture an ocean sunrise.

—Like I said . . . it's just amazing.

—But you've no signal out there?

—Maybe it's amazing *because* there's no signal.

—There's perfectly good software to handle internet addiction, Hugo. Driving to the middle of nowhere: isn't that a bit extreme?

Hugo feels the way he used to feel when his mom drilled him about a new girlfriend: it's not so much that she didn't under-stand the answers, more she didn't even know what questions to ask. He wills Paul to shut up before he says something dangerous. Something unlucky.

—Maybe you need to be there, Paul.

He keeps his voice low but Richie calls from down the table,

—Why don't we all go? It'll be great, I'll bring a bottle of bourbon and a few fishing rods.

Paul looks at Richie then at Hugo, and grins triumphantly. He doesn't brook secrets on the team, likes them all to be one big happy family with himself at head of table. Hugo feels as if something crucial's just left the room but he can't say what. The best he can do is pretend it's all good.

—Sure. Come on down sometime Rich, there's plenty of room.

—Friday's good for me. What do you say?

Richie is quick to push home his advantage, but most of the team are listening to an anecdote about the abysmal viewing stats a rival channel's getting for its big-budget documentary series. Fortunately Paul backtracks.

—Oh wait, no wifi. You know what, Hugo, my weekends are pretty full right now. Some of us can't afford to be offline that long.

BEACH | Come October even surfers are a rarity. Water's too choppy. But whatever the weather Jude and Angelo walk along the shore, just like she's done with every boyfriend she's ever had. It's fine so long as they have their backs to the wind — that way, no sand gets in their eyes — but sooner or later they have to make the turn. Angelo never minds the wind, just narrows his eyes and ploughs right in, sand or no sand. And he'll walk right into the water, even in a storm. Maybe especially in a storm. Power surges excite him, those clashes between sand and water and sky. He gets so close to the breakers he's almost in them, and more than once he's tumbled into the drag, only to scramble ashore on the back of the next wave, grinning and shaking saltwater from his eyes.

—Watch yourself, Angelo. Not the best day for a swim.

That last lazy afternoon up on the dune with Gabriel, everything had appeared so laid back, but afterwards she learned that not far away a couple out swimming off a sand bar had been caught in a freak riptide. It took a while before the beach patrol could get to them. The man made it, his wife did not.

HIGHWAY 158 | The Sunday afternoon sky darkens too soon. The second he's back on the mainland Hugo's phone emits a series of bleeps. A belated notification of three missed calls from the same number: his boss, Paul.

—Hugo? Finally. You in New York?

—Dare County, over the bridge from the island. Just got back in signal.

—Call me when you're in New York.

—It'll be after midnight. But I'm pulled over, I'm good to talk now.

—Forget it, Hugo, I need someone on this right away. I'll talk to your producer instead. He can brief you over breakfast tomorrow.

The line goes dead.

—No need to treat me like a slacker, Paul, just because I take a weekend off.

He shrugs. Best get on. He turns the key in the ignition, restarts the engine, and heads for town. The Outer Banks, with all their quiet magic, stay put.

BEACH | On the dry sands a stray Little Blue scuttles about as if searching for something. Jude knows it's a young bird, for its coat is not solid blue but marbled with white baby feathers. She tries to herd it off the beach.

—Go on back over soundside. You'll probably find your folks in the woodlands. Anyway you'll catch fish easier over there in the still water.

The young heron eyes her, then skitters shorewards, a lame attempt at flight that brings to mind the wind-borne hops of the Wright brothers on Kill Devil Hill. Jude worked summers at the memorial when she was at school, and the old stories about the brothers are so real to her that she still half expects to bump into Orville and Wilbur about the island, plotting how best to control a flying machine, or crash-landing their flimsy glider.

A shrill bleep cuts in: her cell, with a text of her schedule for the rest of the day. Time to go. She persuades a reluctant Angelo to follow.

—Race you to the shower.

They hurtle up the wooden steps to the beach house, leaving a trail of wet sand on the decking. But it's a draw, so they shower together. At her mom's, this could never happen for excess of modesty and want of space, but at Angelo's there are no rules and the shower is a shining waterfall that runs the length of the wet-room. Jude spaces out awhile, rinsing sand and salt from her jeans before peeling them back. She likes to watch sandgrains bank up against the cedarwood sleepers, make a curve, then vanish down the drain. Angelo is done ahead of her and wanders off to catch some sun on the front deck.

She stands by the glass wall watching waves come at her, towel draped loosely around her. The sea air makes her nipples stand proud, but then she often feels sexy up here. The scale of it, maybe. The sense of space. It's the polar opposite of her mom's studio: from where she stands now, the closest neighbour is clear across the ocean in Europe. She rubs herself with the towel then lets it drop. She can walk around stark bollock naked up here and no one will be the wiser.

Except Angelo, and he's not telling.

TV STATION, MANHATTAN | At the canteen Richie is sat behind a plate heaped high with pork. Hugo looks away, barely touches his fruit salad. Given the choice he'd speak to no one but his dog before noon. He taps his fingers while the producer munches bacon, sausages, egg and home fries.

Finally Hugo says,

—So, I heard from Paul last night. Told me something's up. Never said what. You mind filling me in?

Richie mops a scrap of egg yolk from his face.

—Clearances for *Get Real* aren't watertight.

—What?

—Whole bunch of stuff we can't use in the final cut without a bigger fee.

—Who's the troublemaker? I know all the interviewees. One of their lawyers must have cooked this up to boost his percentage.

But when he sees hard copy of the emails bouncing around, Hugo has to admit it's not looking good. Richie ah-hems as if to impart some cultured pearl of wisdom.

—Problem is if we pay the damn fee, costs across the series skyrocket by what, fifteen percent? Won't sit well with Finance. And Paul will go through the roof.

That the best you can offer? Even I got that far, Hugo thinks, while you were still shovelling chunks of sausage into your face. When Richie starts on a *pain au chocolat* and pours another coffee, he gathers up the print-outs.

—Thanks for the heads up Rich. I'll borrow these and talk to someone in legals. Catch you later.

DUNE | After her shift Jude detours to the beach and stretches out on the cool damp sand of the dune, listening to the waves. She has spent so much time in this spot that she can tell with her eyes closed whether a swell is building or the tide is starting to ebb. This is the place where she and Gabriel used to come right through the summer when her shift was over and the Brewing Station had closed for the night. It was the one place they could be alone, away from summer friends and co-workers, away from his family or hers, under the summer stars. It's getting a bit chill for it now but she still loves the empty beach at night: the whispers and moans of the water resonate so strongly that at times she almost feels them herself.

CLAM SHELL DRIVE | When Jude finally gets home she is surprised to find her mom still up. Even more surprised to find she has made supper. Most nights Jude must tiptoe about so as not to wake her or their landlady. The studio is a cheap mother-in-law flat tacked on a large house on Clam Shell Drive, and their rental agreement states noise must be kept to a minimum. Strictly speaking they're not even meant to cook, although they have a microwave and a crock pot. Seeing as her mom's awake Jude grabs the chance for a shower, then pulls on a baggy teeshirt and a pair of denim shorts that are into their third summer, so soft and worn they're only good to wear at home.

Soon as they sit down to eat, it starts.

—Honey, those trainee store manager slots came up again today, so I put your name down. It's time we thought of your future.

Because of her mom's job, Jude ate leftover Subway for lunch right through high school. Mostly egg with cheese as it never sold

133

out. You'd think they'd swap to a flavour people actually liked, but no. Jude never even wants to smell another Subway egg with cheese.

—No way, Mom.

But she doesn't hear. Doesn't want to hear, is the truth.

—Those trainee slots are like gold dust, you get a grounding in . . .

On TV a man in a grey suit is saying surfers can expect challenging conditions late this week while an offshore storm passes by. Scientists can't a hundred percent predict its route, he says, but here's how they think it'll pan out, and the screen cuts to a graphic.

Jude's mom drones on, blocking out his voice.

—Start out right and you won't have to waste years working your way up the ladder, like I did. You can make store manager by the time you're twenty-five.

—I don't want to 'make' store manager, Mom. And I have a job, remember?

Before her mom can say there's no prospects in part-time work, Jude is up and out the door. By the time it reopens spilling a puddle of light on the lawn she is out on the road, her feet falling soundlessly on the sandy edges.

—Jude? Jude!

Silence.

—I know you're out there. You get your ass back in here this second, girl, or I swear I'll lock you out for the night.

The door slams shut and the latch flips on.

A wind stirs the branches of the tall southern oaks. Jude shivers, wishing she'd remembered her jacket. It has her cell in it. Her wallet, too. But she can't go back now. And won't. She walks briskly with no real aim except putting some distance between her and her mom's place. A jingle of loose change comes from her denim shorts and she slips her hand in the pocket to check how much. Not coins, but keys. Two for home, one for her bike padlock, fob for the Brewing Station, and the last? She's blank a minute. Of course. Angelo's. She fingers it, considering. The bar is out of the question, but Angelo has plenty of space and is always pleased to see her. She diverts to collect her pushbike from the back garden, and is on her way.

OFFICE, MANHATTAN | The doctor frowns as he takes the readings, and Hugo feels guilty. The crazy work hours, the erratic diet, the failure to make sufficient down-time: it's all pointed at him like a giant index finger.

—You still have that dog I suggested you get?

—Sure. Thanks again, great idea.

The doctor looks surprised.

—And you walk it every day?

—Right now he's at my summer place. But I get down there most weekends.

A look of surprise, or reproach. Thinks that means the dog is being mistreated? Well, he's wrong.

—I pay a walker to take him out in the week.

A disappointed smile flickers across the doctor's face as he writes out a prescription. Then, when Hugo is halfway out the door,

—I was thinking more of your health than the dog's. You need to look after yourself, Hugo. I can't keep waving a magic wand if you don't do that.

Hugo grimaces in apology and clicks the door shut.

The thing is, Angelo got depressed in the city. His New York walker had so many clients he only went out half an hour a day. Literally a toilet break. The same money now buys a two-mile walk along the shore, feeding and watering, plus the assurance that someone's checking the beach house daily. Which OK, could be done remotely, but it's not the same. Economically, it makes perfect sense. What he left out of the equation when weighing things up is how much he'd miss Angelo, how empty the apartment would feel. He's been going home later and later each night, and because of this he skipped the long drive south last weekend. Add to that another couple of weekends when work got in the way, and it's nearly a month he's not been down. They do video calls every so often, but then he feels bad for treating 'Apple FaceTime' like a thing. He wonders if Steve Jobs did this or if he spent actual time with his kids while he had the chance. But he tries not to think about this too much. It's depressing. Besides, whatever he did or didn't do, Jobs is still one of his heroes.

He tries the walker's number.

Voicemail. Again.

She's been out of contact for days. This is weird. OK, the house is a dead zone, but there's nearly always signal up the beach a ways. Why doesn't she try from there?

BEACH HOUSE | This thing between her and Angelo, it's weird. Three nights, it's only been three nights, but already it's like they live together. Jude can't remember being this comfortable around anyone. Her and Gabriel, she'd been sure for a while there that they got along, but it seems he really wanted something else, someone else. There's her dad, but he went back to Ireland when she was four years old. She remembers a smiling young man with curly hair that she grabbed on to when he carried her high on his shoulders. He sang songs in a crazy falsetto. Mom says that was all he was good for, he never liked hard work.

Her parents were not yet twenty when she was born. Little older than Jude is now. Her father was only really a summer islander who stayed on awhile, and eventually he went back to his own country. Jude has promised herself not to leave. Not yet, anyway. One night when she was fourteen years old she saw the ocean lit up like neon, radiant. White waves scattered diamonds over a black velvet beach. The phosphorescent waves may never return, but Jude wants to see them again, if they do. She has seen a lot of other stuff wash ashore, not all of it good. From Angelo's she has the perfect vantage point.

Clam Shell Drive | When Subway closes for the night Jude's mom goes home and tries to unlock her daughter's phone. She thinks she'll guess the pin code easy, but she's wrong. Five tries and the phone disables itself. Try again in one minute, a message says. Next time she fails to guess it, it tells her try in five minutes. Will it keep locking her out for longer and longer, she wonders, or will it lock her out altogether? Self-destruct somehow. She puts the phone in a cupboard out of sight.

Opening her bag she takes out the tuna and sweetcorn wrap she brought home from work to save cooking dinner. But she's not hungry. She tunes the radio to the local news channel and runs a bath. She has told no one, but she's all messed up about Jude. The night she left, she'd been sure her daughter would return next morning and they'd carry on as normal. But she didn't, and it feels too late to report her missing now. The police will ask why she didn't report it before, what kind of mother is she, they will ask if they argued the night her daughter left. A fact her landlady will confirm, for she hears everything that goes on here: this mother-in-law studio was never properly soundproofed. And if anything's happened to Jude they'll all agree it is her fault. They might even suspect her.

Jude is nineteen years old, she has a job, she's not a child anymore. She can look after herself. The past few days these phrases have run by in her head over and over, like she's rehearsing some future interview or something. She doesn't like to think what.

The bath is full. She turns off the water and dips in a toe. Too hot. She opens a trickle of cold water.

From the other room comes the rhythmic plink-plink-biff of drum, guitar and keyboard. She knows this damn tune by heart. She runs and opens the cupboard door, longing to answer the phone, but without the passcode she cannot. The screen glows in the dark and a man's voice sings, *Enola Gay, you should have stayed at home yesterday . . .*

More keyboard.

Silence, then a small blip that indicates someone has left a message. Who is it that keeps leaving these messages? Is it someone who means harm to her and Jude? Could she contact the police anonymously, post the phone to them, in case they find a way to open it up?

The news station is full of doom and gloom, so she retunes the radio to a music channel before getting in the bath. Once she's finally in she gets the shivers, for under the warm surface the water is colder than it seemed.

SKY | It's a calm night. The fat moon hoists a white road across the water from beach to horizon. A strangely dark patch of sky sits between this white road and the moon. Elsewhere, the sky is light and the sea dark. Of the eleven people on the island who notice this, only two stop to wonder why the sky should be darkest between the moon and its reflection. Jackson and Jude. Jude and Jackson, each staring out at the almost full moon from a different part of the island. But the moon is not telling, it lets them drift off to sleep still puzzling over this mystery.

SOUNDSIDE | The Little Blue feels a hunger-like pang in the night, a sort of nervous fear of leaving the only place it knows. At dawn as it circles its usual spots, the pangs fade. There's a mass of solid grey cloud out to sea. Up above, the sky is a cool blue like it was the day the other Little Blue Herons left. Inland it's bright and sunny: a few fluffy white clouds hurry west, inviting the bird to follow.

The bird flies over the house on Clam Shell Drive where the girl with the long curly hair sometimes leaves out breadcrumbs or scraps of food on a dried-up birdbath. But she hasn't done that for a while now, and there's nothing to be found today either. The door at the side of the house stands open and the Little Blue lands on a bush as if to wait for her to come out, but instead an older, thicker woman emerges, bringing stuff not to the birdbath but to her car: bulging plastic sacks open at the neck, filled with duvets, pillows, clothes, pictures, shoes.

No one else on the street is up yet. The bird darts away, takes a final look at its nest, then swoops off over the water. It does not head towards the sun like its fellow birds did the day that they left, but inland. This way, it has the wind to help it.

BEACH ROAD | Jude takes a spin on her bike first thing to buy paper. She feels self-conscious cycling in her skimpy stay-at-home shorts, for although it's bright there's a cool breeze and it's not really shorts weather at all, as the goosebumps on her legs confirm. She's riding a back road parallel with the oceanfront when a pickup truck overtakes, surfboards loosely piled in back announcing the driver's plan for the day. The driver honks the horn and coasts alongside. Jude turns her head to see who it is. Jackson. Next to him in the front seat two dreadlocked surf dudes a lot younger than him that she knows only by sight, the one near her a boy with soft unshaven cheeks and a scatter of tiny freckles on his nose.

—Gonna be some good breaks the next hour or two. Want to borrow a stick and come with? Chuck that thing in back if you want.

He jerks his chin at her bike, and she thinks how nice it would be to while away the day out on the water.

—Can't. I've got stuff I need to do.

—Your loss. Waves like this don't come often.

Jackson swats an insect off his tanned and tattooed upper arm in a fluid movement that transmutes into a benedictory wave.

—Catch you later, then.

The truck's wheels rasp as it barrels away, raising a cloud of sand and dust that she swerves to avoid. Anyone else and she'd be annoyed, but she knows Jackson's pleasure in motion compels him to make the fastest possible speed between any two given points. And he is oddly likeable in a rogue uncle kind of way, with his hard-man tattoos and his grizzly ZZ Top beard. Shifts at the bar pass swiftly the nights he's there hurling curveball jokes at the other punters, exchanges that are as liable to end in feud as in laughter.

Back at Angelo's Jude has no thoughts for anything but her comic. A few days ago she felt terrified that his owner might come back and find her in his house. She was cleaning up every time she breathed, in case he came back. Now she's convinced he won't be back till Spring, and that meanwhile she may as well make herself at home. She places the fresh paper on the table next to the pages of pencil sketches already done, and pulls out one of those retro vinyl dub reggae numbers that Angelo's owner has in his record collection.

TV STATION, MANHATTAN | What in hell made him think it was a smart move to leave Angelo hundreds of miles away in the care of a total stranger? Hugo checks for another way to reach the dog walker. No land line, no email, nothing. She sent all that in an email, but he's lost it. All he has is her mobile number and her name. Jude.

She's just a teenager. A sweet girl, he thought at the time. But now, who knows? Anything could have happened. She could have left home, got a new job, for all he knows she may have followed some beach boyfriend to New Mexico and brought Angelo with her. Or worse, they may have left him behind to starve. How long would a dog survive without food? Let's say a week. But water. Water is more urgent. And how would a dog locked in a beach house get fresh water to drink?

Hugo shuts down his machine. He finds Paul in the edit suite holding forth to some work placement hopefuls. Fortunately they take a recess for coffee as he arrives.

—Listen Paul, I need to get out of here. It's urgent. Personal stuff.

—This about your beach hut by any chance?

—Close. More about my dog, really. But I do need to get down there.

—You know about the evacuation order?

Hugo stares.

—In Dare County.

—What the . . . What do you mean, evacuation order?

—You really are losing your journalistic touch, aren't you? Hate to be the one to break it to you, but an offshore storm's been upgraded and it's headed straight for North Carolina. Hurricane Silas. This time tomorrow, those beach huts could be history.

The news is like a knee in the balls.

—Look Paul, I need to find my dog. Can you spare me?

—You serious? Your last project came in so far over budget the only way I can spare you is if you shoot me some hurricane footage.

—Sure. Get me a camera and I'll do my best, promise.

—Oh, no. Not your camerawork, you'll need crew.

Hugo goes down to his car to wait. Paul has promised he'll send some gear and a camera operator to the Level 3 underground parking lot in the next ten minutes.

BEACH | This will be the third house this month he's shifted — bit of a run on it this time of year with the storms racing in. Mostly the man works alone, but with the evacuation order, he needs extra help. It's mega-rush: half a dozen move requests came in this week, but he's only got the one trailer. Just as well Jackson and his boys are waiting for him at ten sharp like they said. Their hair's all wet and mussed up like they've been out on the water, and seeing the boards in the pickup, he hopes they don't have no laid-back surfer attitude. He can do without that. The man starts driving and they follow him up the beach, going past a bit of wave damage on the way. A little house is off its stilts and lays there on its side, surf pouring through the windows.

The man stops, unlocks the house they're to move, and they give it a quick once-over.

—OK, guys, so this house and everything in it needs to be on the road in one hour, tops.

A daunting task, and no mistake. For a period beach house it's not small, and it's rammed to the rafters with things that need to be packed up, tied down, or just plain trashed. They'll have to use gut sense, and fast.

Jackson hauls a massive roll of bubble wrap from the truck. The man hands out packing tape dispensers.

—I want the breakables wrapped inside of twenty minutes, we straight? I know that doesn't give much time but it's how it is.

—We're on it.

—And anything that's a hazard, get rid. You with me?

—Yup.

The rip of plastic forms an off-kilter riff that blends with the arrhythmic soundtrack of surf and gusts of wind. Hearing it, the man feels calmer as he travel-proofs the rooms. These boys may look a mite strange, but they're good to work with. Don't talk much, but they get stuff done.

CREEK, ALBEMARLE SOUND | Across the sound in a straight line there's no end to the water, so instead the Little Blue makes a series of shorter hops around the creeks, until it spies a thin strip of land projecting across the sound. Two strips in fact, right next to each other: one clogged with cars, one empty. It flies above them a stretch.

It's a cool, energetic day, still sunny though a bank of grey cloud draws closer. From time to time galloping clouds cast their shadows so the water beneath goes from bright and sparky to a dull khaki-ish green. When the bird tires, it perches on the empty land strip for a rest. Even from here the car noise is powerful and, soon as it can, it takes off again, the wind lifting it on its way. The Little Blue feels light and strong, as if it could fly forever.

TV STATION, MANHATTAN | Hugo is in the underground parking lot when he gets a text from News asking him to bring the car to reception. He swears softly as he puts it in gear. Shafts of light scissor between tall buildings like the opening scene of a movie as for once he drives around the block in under ten minutes. A fresh-faced cameraman loads his gear in the car, then takes a seat in back.

—Oli.

Hugo thinks that means hello, maybe in Portuguese?

—The passenger side is free.

—Not what they told me.

—We got someone else coming?

—Presenter. Newsreader or something.

—Well they better be here soon.

Hugo glances at the time, checks the storm warning feed. It hasn't changed. *Landfall expected NC coast late aft/early eve, exact time unknown.* He half turns in his seat to see the cameraman. Hard to tell for sure coming from the grand old age of forty-three, but he'd put him at somewhere between eighteen and twenty-five.

—You done any storm reporting? Or storm chasing?

—Uh-uh. I'm on work experience. But major news events is an area I really want to get into.

Newsdesk has a lot to answer for, chucking a trainee at an assignment like this. But now is not the moment to bring that up, especially when the passenger door opens and Paul gets in.

—Good, I see you and Oliver have met. Talented young fellow. Oli, I bet Hugo hasn't said, but he's a senior director in Factual. He also has a beach house on the Outer Banks, so he doubles as your human interest angle.

Hugo bristles. If he's to be the subject of the shoot, first he's heard. But he'll fight that battle when it comes to it.

—Uh, Paul?

—Yup.

—Why are you in my car?

—Didn't you know? I'm on back to shop floor.

—And they cleared you to spend time on this?

—Yup. Right after they upped my key man insurance. Nice, huh?

—Lovely. Like poker, they just doubled on you!

—Who cares. Let's show 'em how to file a news report, eh Hugo. Take me back to my foreign correspondent days.

Hugo's heard Paul's foreign correspondent tales before and frankly he's more than a bit worried they'll be revisited now for Oli's benefit. The journey's long enough without that. To keep things nice and steady he picks the Velvet Underground, the one with the banana on the cover, and 'Sunday Morning' starts to play.

BEACH HOUSE | Angelo is restless when she settles to her drawing. She can't blame him really, but she wants to get this done. She has a whole eight-page comic she wants to draw and colour, that she's promised to a friend for his 'zine, and Saturday is copy day.

—Give me half an hour Angelo, then we'll go out, OK?

He makes a small dissatisfied sound, but Jude cannot help it: she wants to ink all her outlines in one go, if she can. It's the only way she knows of to get the people in her strip to look the same from one frame to the next. She pulls on her employer's chunky sound mixing headphones and turns up the volume.

He wanders away sadly. The extensive collection of period dub reggae keeps Jude working full tilt, and blocks out both Angelo's pleas to her and the insistent rush of the incoming tide. From time to time Angelo nudges her foot. When he gets no reaction he takes up a spot under the desk where he can be sure to know about it the moment she takes a break.

Even here he's restless, and not your standard Angelo kind of restless. More anxious than that. Sort of festery.

Jude feels mean for changing his schedule and ignoring him, but this is a one-off. A day when she has priority. What's stressing Angelo out, she guesses, is the fact he's not getting his usual *numero uno* treatment.

HIGHWAY 13 | Hugo stops to refill the tank, and when he's paid up he finds one of his passengers has gone missing. Eventually Paul reappears, carrying a box that fills the car with the scent of warm fat and sugar.

—Try one, they're amazing.

—Had you down as more of a gourmet type, Paul.

—My wife has flat out banned *churritos* at home. Guess that's why car journeys without her are so enjoyable.

Paul munches quickly as if the nest of fried dough snakes is a piece of work he urgently has to get through. Hugo wishes Oliver would help keep Paul amused, but a glance in the rear-view mirror confirms he's dozing again. No wasted adrenaline there.

—Are you sure there isn't a faster route? At this rate we'll be lucky to find any hurricane left.

—The drive south often takes seven to eight hours. Do it at night and you maybe knock an hour off it.

But Paul doesn't seem to believe him, for if he's not balancing food on his touchscreen device, he's looking up alternate routes or modes of transport they could have used to reach Kill Devil Hills more swiftly.

—Say we flew into Norfolk out of JFK and rented a car: JFK-Charlotte, Charlotte-Norfolk. That's four or five hours on the flights, plus a drive either side.

—Plus airport wait time.

—No, you're right, forget it. Let's see, how about Suffolk? No, the Great Dismal Swamp is bang in our way . . . How the hell do people reach the Outer Banks?

—You know me, I drive every time.

Hugo is thinking he should call his dog walker again. If she and Angelo were evacuated, she'll be in signal. Except he can't call, not this second, because Highway 13 is giving way to the awesome splendour of the Chesapeake Bay Bridge, an engineering power trip he's convinced was dreamt up by a rich hippy architect from Cape Charles: *Hey man, why don't we build a bridge right over to Norfolk, with tunnels for the yachts to sail in and out, and a few man-made islands to keep the whole thing afloat?* Only in the 1960s. These days the save the dolphins crowd would block it at source. Driving across it is like driving into the sea, so much so that he sometimes can't see far in front of his nose. They cut the speed limit when the weather's poor, or shut it down. Even when conditions are perfect its seventeen-mile slalom of hills, bends and tunnels puts Hugo on edge, and right now the overhead signs are warning 'the max safe speed is 30mph'. Which means they'll be on the bridge half an hour instead of fifteen minutes. Compared to this, crossing the three-mile Wright Memorial Bridge to the Outer Banks is a piece of cake.

BEACH HOUSE | As Jude turns off the music and gets up to clear the table, a hard rain whips up out of nowhere, sucking the light from the sky.

—Not the best moment, eh Angelo? Sorry, we should've gone out for your walk sooner.

But rain or no rain he needs the walk so she grabs a coat belonging to his owner and opens the screen door.

—You coming?

Angelo charges along the deck and down the steps. The last few steps are underwater and he has to swim across. Jude splashes after him, excited. The water's only knee deep so it's not scary, it's fun, and the push of the gale is fun too. The day she interviewed for this job, Angelo's owner told her that once a decade a spring tide pushes water up past the house. He pulled out the unused inflatable life raft secured to the deck railings, and laughed. The last owners must have bought it for its conversation value, he said, because my neighbours tell me the tideline's never come up past the first set of stilts. How amazing then to stay here just a few days and witness this.

From the shrunken beach she looks where the surfers usually hang: no one. Rip's too strong even for Jackson. The waves are huge but messily formed, each roiling into the last instead of advancing in neat parallels the way they usually do. And not only are the surfers absent, there is no one out walking either.

Just up the shore she sees a gap where a beach house has been towed away, only a few posts left to mark the fact it ever stood there. Its neighbours, left to face the oncoming waves, have the grim look of reluctant front-line soldiers. She's trying to work out if the missing house is Gabriel's when there's a screech as the roof metal peels off the house next in line and hurtles around in the air like a plastic bag, before crashlanding in the dunes. Clothes, toys, even a chair erupt out of the rafters, then twist away like sparks from a bonfire.

A sudden spike in wind intensity and Jude finds herself flat in the sand, her borrowed coat half off and flapping about her head. The background roar of an approaching jet plane confuses her. It must have drifted a long way off course, because there's only a small unmanned airfield here, for light aircraft. For a moment she's fearful it's coming down right here on the beach, but when she glances up quickly just in case, there *is* no plane. Just the noise of the wind. This is not just a spring tide storm, she realises: they have to take shelter, now.

She would run back to the beach house for her bike and her drawings, but already the water around the house looks deep, too deep for Angelo. Tomorrow will have to do. High tide's not for what, a few hours, so the sea will keep coming. It has dispensed with all regular consensus on where the boundaries lie, and is intent on a land grab. Anyone stupid enough to leave boats, cars, bicycles, even houses in its way, is fair game.

Jude calls Angelo. But he is one step ahead of her: waiting up at the top of the sands, itching to get on the road and out of here. His mouth opens and closes repeatedly, his urgent barked exhortations lost in the rush of the gale.

SOUNDSIDE | The trees are dancing. Supple young trees that can bend from the waist get off lightly. Those that cannot keep pace with the wind groan in protest. But this is not the kind of wind who takes no for an answer: this wind is an emperor who wants the whole world to dance to his tune, for whom there is no future, no past, only the imperative present. Light on their feet, the deciduous trees gamely shrug off the encumbrance of their final few leaves and dance in their lacy winter coats, losing nothing more than the odd twig here and there. The evergreens are less fortunate; their greenery creates resistance, and once a frond snaps off it is gone for good. Even the small trees and bushes near the sound, summer home to a colony of Little Blue Herons, do not escape the wind's attention. The littlest Little Blue left the island only this morning. Just in time, for now his nest is unravelled into its constituent twigs and pitched across the sound in his wake.

WRIGHT MEMORIAL BRIDGE | It's only three o'clock but it's dusk by the time they finally reach the bridge to the Outer Banks. It shouldn't be dark this early, Hugo says. Paul brightens and says it must be storm darkness. Oli seems nervous at this, but gets his camera out in case he needs to start shooting. Waiting in line at the police road block ahead of the bridge, Paul, in the passenger seat, swiftly assesses the situation: the only vehicles being waved through from mainland to island are emergency services. He hisses at Oli to hide his camera. When they're beckoned to the front, he rolls down his window and briefly flashes ID at the officer.

—We got clearance as part of the weather service, we're scientists deployed to record wind speeds over at Kitty Hawk.

The big bosses over at the National Hurricane Centre reckon tonight is going to set a few records.

Hugo blows his nose to keep from letting out a yelp of laughter, but amazingly, the officer waves them through.

—Rather you than me.

When the police officer is well behind them, Hugo high-fives Paul.

—What? We are going to record stuff. Near enough.

One of the twin two-laners is shut for repairs, so the remaining bridge is in two-way use. The traffic is nearly all against them, people leaving the island in cars, SUVs and small vans. Paul voices his irritation.

—Didn't think Outer Banks folk would heed an evacuation. Figured they were more the sort to ride it out.

—When the going gets tough, take action. If things go wrong you might not have time to change your mind.

PICKUP | It's addictive, watching the waves. All three of them have had a go at recording footage on their phone cameras, keeping close to the beach houses so they'd have something to hang on to if they fell. Even so they got soaked and pummelled by the waves, and Jackson damn near lost his phone, so now they're drying off while they keep watch from inside the truck. Earlier, they shifted the wooden house from the shoreline before the waves hit, but failed to relocate it as a section of highway they needed to cross was flooded. The islands, being essentially one huge sandbank system, are fairly flat, so a bit of extra water goes a long way. Just minutes ago Jackson had to back up the truck because the sea rose up and started pounding the hell out of the Virginia Dare Trail. Right now it's doing its best to rearrange the shore-front houses at odd angles or wash them out to sea. Jackson is mesmerised. This is the highest he's ever seen the waves, he says, not taking his eyes off them for a second. They're all three wondering if the water will ever recede, or if the polar ice has finally melted and has raised sea levels across the planet.

—Makes you think, doesn't it . . .

—Makes you think what?

—You know, about climate change and stuff.

—Here's what I think about climate change, dude. I don't even want to think about it, just like everyone else.

—I know it.

They do not look at one another when they speak, just keep staring out the windshield as if at their very own disaster movie. The boy with the tiny freckles averts his face from it and says:

—Stuff like that, it's too big to get our heads around. Right now we need to focus on the little stuff staring us in the face.

The others turn to him, silent.

—Stuff like, should we still be sitting here when any moment a piece of roof metal or a tree could crush the cab, and us with it? Should we be anywhere near these waves, because if ever there's a time when a freak wave looks likely, this is it, so maybe we should wait this one out further back from the front line.

His companions look at the freckle-faced boy with respect. He may be the youngest, but he has a brain and he's not afraid to use it. Jackson, putting the truck in gear, attempts to salvage a sense of leadership.

—Good thinking, Bones. So: the Jolly Roger, or the movie theatre?

—No glass windows to shatter at the movie theatre.

—I like it. I could use me some fresh popcorn.

BEACH ROAD | The road is an actual beach now, clumps of sand all over it. In a few places she can still see bits of road surface: jagged curves of it broke loose and jumbled up, like a giant toffee slab that's been cracked open.

—This is serious, Angelo. First off we need a solid concrete wall and a strong roof between us and this wind.

Angelo barks keenly in reply.

Jude thinks of the movie complex. It's far enough from shore that it won't get wet, and when the wind drops she can cross the highway from there to Clam Shell Drive, and check on her mom. But the wind doesn't seem as if it will be dropping any time soon. Jude looks behind her and gets a shock. These last waves have so much reach, there's almost no sand left. Seawater swarms up the gaps between the houses, seemingly unstoppable.

She and Angelo make a run for it.

They stay clear of trees because out in the open they've a chance to see what's coming before it hits them. They cut through by the Jolly Roger, its windows gaffer-taped with X's and the doors sandbagged, past the lagoon which is looking about ready to join up with the sea. That's when she hears the pickup trailing her across the grass.

—Jude, Jude, get in. Quick before the door blows off!

It's Jackson and the two boys she saw with him this morning, such a long time ago. A powerful gust shakes out the dumpster behind the restaurant, sending gnawed chicken wings flying into the air. Jude hurries in and sits in the middle, Angelo scrambles after her and tries to sit on her knees. The skinny boy by the door scoots up to shut it. The noise drops once he finally gets it closed, but they still have to shout to be heard.

—How come you're still here, Jude? Why haven't you been evacuated?

—You could have said something about that when we met. I didn't know about any evacuation.

Jude pushes Angelo off her, and he retaliates by shaking sand and off his wet fur.

—I thought everyone knew . . .

—Never mind.

—Sorry. Some news to miss, huh!

—First I knew was when this guy's house got flooded, hey Angelo. But if everyone's evacuated, why're *you* here?

Jackson grins sheepishly.

—Bit of freelance. We loaded up this house to shift it to a new plot. Sure glad the dude that hired us paid cash upfront, because the road was shot to hell, sand and water all over. Now he's driving around looking for a safe place to park up the house where it won't get trashed.

—Nowhere's safe, dude, it's a hurricane.

WRIGHT MEMORIAL BRIDGE | Halfway over, a slow patch up ahead becomes a full stop. Every so often a gap ripples down the road, but mostly nothing moves. Hugo eases his car along.

Tough being so near and yet so far, and it doesn't help that Paul is dozing beside him like a sugar-sleepy child who has stopped believing they'll ever arrive, waking every so often to ask are they nearly there yet (or in Paul's case, if there's any sign of that goddamn hurricane). Gradually Hugo becomes aware what's causing the problem: a trailer full of household goods being towed off the island is taking up not just the oncoming lane, but a good part of the outbound lane too.

When Paul wakes they're close enough to the trailer to see the wind doing its best to unpack it. So far, the trailer's standing up to the buffeting. Paul decides it's time for Oliver to get some footage.

—That's a good visual, Oli, you getting it?

—I'm trying.

—Well, go on. Step out the car why don't you, get a proper angle on it. And record some of that wind noise too, will you?

Paul appears to be staying put, so Hugo offers to help.

—I can hold a light for you. Traffic's so jammed up it makes no difference.

So long as they're in the car with the music on, the storm is a big bad thing out there from which the twin miracles of gas and electricity preserve them. But as soon as they get out, a shower of blue sparks goes off like a giant firework, and the lights on the bridge fail.

Instantly, all sense of immunity dissipates.

While Oli's filming, Hugo phones the dog walker again. It's a genius idea. This time, not only does the call connect, but a second later he can actually hear her phone ringing somewhere nearby. Hugo hears the tune only for a few seconds before the combined audio force of waves and wind drown it out: *E-no-la Gay* . . . But with a ringtone like that, a few seconds is enough. He knows it by heart because one weekend she left her phone in his house by accident, and it rang about twenty times before she collected it the next day.

—Angelo! Angelo, you hear me?

He shines the portalight on stopped cars as he tries to locate the source of the ringtone. But he can't see Angelo or his walker. He calls again, and this time follows the sound until he's closer: *Eno-la Gay, it should have never had to end this way, A-ha* . . . Just his luck, the shore-bound traffic picks this moment to surge forward.

Everything happens very quickly after that. A huge noise

and a rocking underfoot at the same time, and in the dark Hugo hasn't a clue if it's an earthquake or what. He looks at where the screeching metal sounds are coming from, yells, 'Oli, Paul, run!' and is out of there. He runs right past the ringtone car, seeing in a blur its sole occupant, an image played back in his head later when the screams have all died down, when he has forced his way between the lines of cars and back to shore.

Standing among a crowd of people who also left the bridge, wearing shiny metallic blankets given them by some well-meaning first aider, Hugo doesn't think to protest when a news crew starts to film him. He's numb. Lost in a silent world in which he sees and hears the same things, over and over. One minute he's driving his car; the next he doesn't even know if he still has a car. In between, the blue sparks of the transformer blowing out, the ringtone, the search for Angelo, the screech of torn metal as the span gives way, the lit-up scared face of the middle-aged woman driver, the car horns and shouts and screams all mixed in with the wind and the beat of his heart . . . Hugo is not a good interviewee, he does not answer the reporter's questions. He doesn't even hear them.

He hopes Paul and Oli are safe. He can't see them, hasn't yet had a reply from Paul, but that doesn't prove they are casualties. Possibly they got across to Kill Devil Hills. The dredger hit near where the car was stopped. But this much he knows: if anyone has staged a miraculous escape, it is Paul. The man has always been lucky. With his talent for the ratings game, luck is how he made a living. Makes, not made. How he makes a living.

KILL DEVIL HILLS | Overnight, water washes over practically the whole of the Outer Banks, except the raised bits. (Which in fact are not raised so very high: what passes for a hill in these parts is barely a hummock elsewhere.) The flood waters may not be deep but they have a tenacious pull, knocked over the older or more fragile wooden buildings and dragging them into the waves. Many sections of road are pulled to pieces: the road itself may be durable, but the onslaught of water steals the ground from under it until it buckles or breaks under its own weight. It's as if the island wants to soften the hold of the man-made grid that covers its surface, perhaps even stage a return to the pristine state it was in not so very long ago. Each time the waves wash over the land, fewer man-made objects, fewer straight lines, are left in their wake. But concrete doesn't wash off easy, and the elevated highways that skirt the shorelines of the islands and form bridges between them show no sign of being washed away. These long sandbanks may vanish underwater and the herons find new places to nest, a long time before that happens.

KC Movie Theatres | The cinema is one of the few places with its own back-up power generator, something they didn't know when they chose it, but which comes in damn useful. Because of this, it's a magnet for anyone still left on the island. The elevators are stuck and the entrance hall got a bit wet, but the building got off lightly compared to some of its neighbours.

The skinny, freckle-faced boy, Bones, is up early. Before anyone else is awake he has set up a kitchen in the popcorn shop on the first floor foyer, where he stays all morning, making coffee and tea. Later he sends Jackson on an expedition to the nearest shop for supplies so he can keep on doling out tea, coffee and cinema snacks, and also make something a bit more food-like, such as soup. His 'customers' are dazed people with sodden trousers and muddy socks who arrive at the cinema and attach their mobile phones to any power socket they can find that is still functioning.

Jude goes shopping with Jackson on condition he detours to her mom's place, round the corner at Clam Shell Drive. When they get there the doors to the studio stand open, swollen with the influx of sand and silt. Pretty much every sign that anyone ever lived here is gone. Jude is distraught, leaving Jackson in the unfamiliar role of providing the voice of reason.

—Jude, listen. For sure, your mom packed up and left before this hit . . .

—We don't know that, no one saw her leave.

—I sure did. Left in a hurry, no time to inform me.

Jude knows this thin, insistent voice: it belongs to the landlady, whom she thinks of as 'the witch'.

—Never even offered me a lift, like a good neighbour would have done.

Jude follows the voice outside to the garden. The old lady is on the steps leading to the first floor, outside the big door leading to her own quarters in the main house.

—You saw her leave? When?

—Yesterday morning, quite early. Why, you're the daughter, aren't you?

—That's right.

—Do tell me your new address, there may be letters I need to pass on.

It's clear she means bills.

—Don't have one. I stayed at the movie theatre last night. And I don't know where my mom's gone either.

Jude trails off on a high note, suddenly close to tears. She looks away at the house, and notes that the mud line does not reach as far as the old lady's quarters: her own home is unscathed, and here she is worrying about extracting more money from her mom.

Jackson steps in:

—Yes, there's a group of us at the cinema. We've still got power there. Maybe you'd like to join us, ma'am?

In the end the old lady thanks him for the invitation, but says she'd prefer to be in her own home even without electricity. She allows Jackson to add her details to a list of people to be contacted should the situation get worse, or should the electricity not be restored in a few days.

When they return to the cinema a young man with a video camera is interviewing anyone who will talk to him about the events of last night. He's only about Jude's age, but he seems to work for a TV station. Jude asks which one, and he says anyone that will pay. He asks if she'll talk and she hesitates, then says yes. Angelo curls up next to her while she gives the interview.

—My mom left on the evacuation, and we didn't have time to talk before she went. So, Mom, if you're watching this, I'm fine, I'm at the movie theatre. I hope you're good, get in touch when you can, yeah?

When he's stopped filming, Oli asks Jude,

—You are alright, aren't you?

—Yeah sure. At least I have Angelo on my side. My guardian angel . . . I could have drowned if it wasn't for him.

—Angelo?

—Yeah, that's right. My dog. Why?

—Oh, nothing. Just, I met this guy before . . . I was with him on the bridge filming when the spans in the middle collapsed . . . I thought, but I might be wrong . . . Anyway, uh, I don't think he made it.

Jude is quiet. Whatever happened on the bridge, she would almost prefer not to hear about it. Later, when the reporter is editing his footage, she cuddles Angelo.

—It's just us two now. I'll look after you.

DUNE | It's a few days later when the sort of dazzling sun arrives that often comes right on the heels of a storm. A day when everything is clear and bright. The daylight hours go by swiftly because everyone has outdoor work to do; with the rain that followed, this is the first real chance since the hurricane to do any clearing up.

Jude is living in a disused projection room at the movie theatre. Jackson is sort of half there, half moved back to his own place. The water's drained out of his house and he has lots of cleaning to do, but he's lucky. Apparently it's going to be habitable. His latest quip is: Lucky I couldn't afford an oceanfront house, though it's a dang sight closer to the ocean than it was.

In the early evening, Bones screens a film on a donation basis, as a benefit for the flood repair effort. The movie theatre's contacted him to say they have can stay on until the bridges are reopened and mains power to the island is restored. After the movie, Jude helps him clear up, and they take Angelo on a nighttime walk to the ocean, using the 'ferry', two small boats on a pulley system that Jackson rigged up for getting across the lagoon and back to his place. For some reason the water's sticking in this area. Busted storm drain is what Bones thinks, and Jude has no idea if he's right, or if it's a permanent coastline shift. Overhead, the sky is calm and bright, filled with the most amazing stars.

—I'm not sure it's a popular view, but . . .

—But what?

—I almost prefer the island this way. Without street-lights, there are so many stars. And it's so quiet you can hear the waves all over.

—You mean, like it used to be? Before people came along.

—More like itself, I guess. Or how it could be, if we didn't need so much stuff.

He says nothing, just watches and listens. She likes that about him, how she almost imagines she can hear him thinking but then he'll come out and say something she would never have predicted. They walk in a close little group, Angelo noticeably more cautious than usual, sticking close to Jude instead of running off adventuring. They come at the shoreline from a point where the dunes are high, so as not to get waterlogged. At least that's the plan. They have to watch their step all the same. The beach has not fully reappeared and no one knows yet if it will do, or if the sands and waters have shifted to a new equilibrium.

—Sorry. I guess that's a terrible thing to say. I just mean, well, when things get back to normal here . . .

—If . . .

—If, whichever. Well, me and Angelo, we've been thinking we might move on. Go visit some quieter islands for a while. Belize, or Chile maybe.

Just then they come up over the hump of the last dune and in sight of the water, which is green and frothy. The rollers tonight are so long and straight they're like trains, but the most striking thing is the phosphorescence: how it softly illuminates each breaker from beneath, and how each shining wave lumbers up the steep-banked sand only to smash in a brilliant neon spray at the foot of the dune, just below them. Jude is quiet then, they all are.

They watch the neon waves for long minutes, maybe for

hours. Somewhere under those waves is Angelo's house, and with it her bicycle, what's left of her drawings and the dub reggae records she was listening to before all this happened. It seems weeks ago, not days. By the time they start back towards the cinema the moon is slipping, and Jude knows that if she and Angelo do move on, chances are Bones will come with them. She is first across the dunes, and so when the others catch up she stands in the front of the boat and pulls on the rope. It is late into the night, that time after the moon is done when the stars burn brighter than ever, making little points of light in the still water ahead of her as well as in the sky above.

A Note on the Author

Lane Ashfeldt grew up in Dublin where she went to school and university. After failing a job interview for the Irish Civil Service, she worked in the Parnell Mooney, in factories and as a news-website and radio journalist before starting to write fiction. Her short fiction has been published in literary magazines and journals in Ireland, England, Greece and the US. Her stories have appeared in several anthologies, from *Punk Fiction* (Portico) to the rather more genteel *Dancing With Mr Darcy* (Honno/HarperCollins US). This début collection of short fiction contains a dozen or so short stories inspired by the sea, among them stories awarded first place in the Fish Short Histories prize and the Global Short Stories prize. Lane Ashfeldt is a fellow of the International League of Conservation Writers, and a Hawthornden Fellow.

www.ashfeldt.com